The Girl Who Moved *to the* Town That Wasn't There

The Hlavka Family,

Enjoy the history!

[signature]

Siouxland Heritage Museums
200 W. 6th Street
Sioux Falls, SD 57104
museum@minnehahacounty.org
www.siouxlandmuseums.com

Printed and bound in the United States of America

First Edition

10 9 8 7 6 5 4 3 2 1

LCCN 2020911136
ISBN 978-0-578-71305-2

This book was proudly produced by Book Bridge Press.
www.bookbridgepress.com

The Girl Who Moved *to the* Town That Wasn't There

by Suzanne Hovik Fuller
illustrations by Emmeline Forrestal

SIOUXLAND HERITAGE MUSEUMS
Sioux Falls • South Dakota

Dedicated with gratitude to pioneer newspaper editors W.S. Cobban and George Lanning, who reported the founding and first year of Egan, Dakota Territory, 1880–1881, in *The Egan Express.*

With sincere thanks to the following people who helped me move this story forward:

Linda Hasselstrom
Eric Braun
Dale Johnson
Bill Hoskins
Kyle Wigg
Sandy Rogin
Robert Kolbe
Dr. Ed Harvey
Jo Vaughn Gross
Jean Nicholson

Sandra Ladegaard
Joy Bartlett
Ginger Smith
Susan McAdaragh
Ruth Metcalf
Beth Jensen
Katie Jensen
Krista Fuller
Larry Fuller
Sophia Fuller

Janet Stverak and her 4th and 5th grade students, who read and gave feedback on early drafts of the manuscript in 1999.

Contents

1880
May

First Chapter of a New Year

Monday, May 3

Virgie froze, her fork halfway to her mouth.

She heard just three words.

"We are moving."

Part of her mind heard Papa's proud voice happily announcing, "I've taken a new job! I'll be the grain buyer in Egan, about 40 miles north of here." Railroads were expanding westward into Dakota Territory, and towns like Egan were being built along the new routes. Papa said after he found a house for them, they would move.

But the rest of Virgie's mind was reeling at the thought of leaving her friends, of leaving Sioux Falls. Her stomach churned. Her eyes filled with tears. She put down her fork, stood up, and said, "May I be excused?" Without waiting for the answer, she ran out the back door.

Sobbing, she ran across the empty dirt field to the Carnahan house. The Carnahan twins, Carrie and Catherine, had been her best friends since both families moved to Sioux Falls four years ago.

"We're moving!" Virgie blurted out. The three ten-year-olds sat down on the front step, and Virgie told them everything. With arms around each other, they cried. Virgie wiped away the tears with the sleeve of her dress. "I just had an idea," she said. "Remember Sigrid Olsen? When her family moved, she stayed here and lived with the Johansens."

"That's right," Carrie said. "Maybe you could stay and live with us. Let's ask Ma." All three girls ran inside the house. "Could Virgie live with us when her family moves?" asked Carrie and Catherine at the same time.

"What's this?" Mrs. Carnahan said. The girls told her Virgie's news. "Oh, my," Mrs. Carnahan said, wiping her flour-dusted hands on her brown gingham apron. "Let's sit down and talk about this," she said as she pulled up a chair. "Virgie's parents would miss her terribly. And she would miss them. Besides, where would we put another body? This house is barely big enough for the ten of us. Virgie needs to be with her family."

Virgie knew Mrs. Carnahan was right. She would miss her family. But that didn't make the thought of leaving Carrie and Catherine any easier. She slowly walked back home.

Mama, hands on her hips, was standing by the door when Virgie walked in. "Why did you run out?" Mama asked.

"I don't want to move," Virgie said. "After I told Carrie and Catherine we were going to move, they asked their Ma if I could live with them."

The straight line of Mama's mouth softened as she looked at her younger daughter. "Oh, dear. We could never let you stay. We would miss you too much." Mama put her arm on Virgie's shoulder and led her to the parlor settee. "I know this is hard. My family moved from New York to Wisconsin to Minnesota. And when Papa moved us to Sioux Falls, I had to leave my sisters and brother. I know all about saying goodbye to family and friends." She gave Virgie a hug as they stood up. "This is a good job for Papa. The whole family is moving, Virginia." Virgie knew the discussion was closed.

After breakfast the next morning, Mama said, "Girls, would you please help Papa bring packing barrels into the kitchen and the parlor?" Virgie and her fourteen-year-old sister Ruth went to the barn with Papa, tipped the heavy barrels on their sides, and rolled them to the house.

When the wooden barrels were lined up in the kitchen, Mama directed the packing of kitchen items that would not be needed in the next two weeks. Then they went upstairs to the girls' bedrooms.

"You girls pack up your own rooms," Mama said. "Virgie, the doll and toy tea set from Grandmama should travel safely in one of the round-top trunks."

"Will Ruth and I each have our own bedroom in our new house?" Virgie asked.

"We'll have to see what Papa finds," Mama said.

Papa came up the stairs and stopped at the doorway. "You girls are going to have a job packing up everything," he said, shaking his head. "I'm leaving in a few minutes," he added.

Papa was on his way to the town of Roscoe, which was being abandoned because the railroad had moved its route away from the town. With no trains coming through, people and goods could not move in and out of town. That's why the settlers were building a new town—Egan—on the new route where the train tracks would soon be put down. The prairie offered limited supplies of lumber, and there were no trains yet to bring in building materials. So the pioneers made do with what was available—the houses and businesses sitting in Roscoe. People were selling their houses to be moved whole to Egan. Papa was going to Roscoe to buy one for his family.

Mama walked out the door with Papa as he went to his horse, Dusty. "Aggie," he said quietly, "I realize what a risky move this is for us. We're going out on an empty, open prairie where people hope to build a town. There's no guarantee this town succeeds. I'm excited about this chance to be the head buyer. But weather and grasshoppers can affect the wheat and corn crops. We're facing a challenge. I'm going to do everything I can to make this move a success, but let's agree that we'll give it a year to make it work for our family. "

Mama reached over and patted his hand. "I'll agree to that," she said.

For the next two weeks, Virgie and Ruth helped Mama pack. As they worked, Mama often talked about the things they were taking along. She picked up the Seth Thomas clock. "This was a wedding gift to my parents when they were married in 1843 in upstate New York. The family has taken it to Wisconsin, Minnesota, and now Dakota Territory," she said as she unhooked the pendulum. "The family has been good caretakers of it. Someday one of you will have it."

Virgie and Ruth looked at each other. "I don't like these conversations," whispered Virgie to Ruth. "I don't want to think of Mama and Papa dying."

Ruth nodded. "I know," she said, "but that's Mama. She wants to make sure we know about family things." Mama wrapped the pendulum and key in a soft cloth, and then the girls helped lift the clock into a barrel and place the pendulum next to it. They padded the clock with crocheted afghans from the parlor settee and chairs.

Next, Virgie picked up the brass-framed mirror from a

table. She looked at her reflection in the mirror. Light blue eyes stared back at her. Her eyebrows always had a slight quizzical upturn. Straight light brown hair hung down her back past her thin shoulders and was held away from her pale face by a thin ribbon. *My,* she thought. *How serious I look. Do I always look like that, or is it because I'm sad that we are moving?*

Before she could continue that thought, her sister's dark brown eyes and big smile crowded into the frame. "I need to pull this hair out of my face," she said as she took a ribbon and gathered her thick, wavy chestnut brown hair up and back.

Their conversation was interrupted by a knock at the door.

Mama answered. "Mrs. Carnahan! Good morning. Come in for a cup of tea."

"Thank you, Mrs. Vandenberg," Mrs. Carnahan said. "I can't stay. I have to go back to the children, but I wanted to pass on a tip I learned from our last move: Put your cream in a small tin pail, cover it, and tie it onto your wagon. The motion will churn the cream into butter. Thank you for being such good neighbors. We wish you all the best."

When most of the packing was finished, Virgie turned her thoughts to her friends.

"Mama," she said, "I want to give Catherine and Carrie something to remember me by. But I can't think of anything."

"Well," Mama said, "I have a couple of items to buy at the store, so let's see what's there."

As they walked down the dirt road, they could hear hammers echoing across town as workers built yet another store or house. They passed the two-story brick Central School building. "I wonder what my new school will look like," Virgie said as she looked at the sun reflecting off the empty windows.

Downtown, Mama was greeted by several women who wished her good luck in the move.

Virgie glanced across the street as she heard, over it all, the screechy metallic sound of rollers as merchants on the east side of the street unfurled canvas awnings to protect the windows of their stores from the afternoon sun.

They passed general stores, restaurants, grocers, a confectionary, saloons, law offices, loan offices, real estate offices, and a pawn office. A store sign promised, *Highest cash price paid for hides, furs, wool, pelts, and tallow.*

They stopped at a general store. Shelves lining the walls held the latest in household items, clothing, and dry goods. Virgie peered at an item in a glass case along the aisle.

"That red velvet one with the girl on the cover is pretty. What kind of book is it?" she asked the clerk.

"It's an autograph book," the clerk replied. "All the girls back east are buying them. Friends sign their names on the blank pages."

"Oh, can I buy it?" Virgie asked her mother, who nodded.

At home, Virgie carefully signed her name and the date, May 16, 1880, on its first page.

Virgie handed it to Ruth, who signed her name and wrote, "Destiny is not without thee, but within; Thyself must make thyself."

Virgie walked over to Carrie and Catherine's house. "Thank you!" Carrie said as she opened to the first page. Catherine added, "We'll get lots of autographs."

In return, the twins gave Virgie a book of *Andersen's Fairy Tales*. "Oh," Virgie said. "You know how I love reading. This is perfect."

Monday, May 17

Just before supper, Virgie heard a noise and looked outside to see Papa standing next to a wagon and two oxen. "Papa's home!" she shouted as she ran out the door.

"After I saw all the packing going on, I decided the wagon was going to be too heavy for the horses to pull, so I bought these two oxen," he said. "I'll tell you more over supper. It smells like we're having fried chicken. I'm ready to eat!"

As they finished their meal, he said, "It was a long two weeks, but I have good news! I found a nice house in Roscoe and had it moved to Egan. You'll be happy to know you girls will each have your own bedroom." He told them their new home was ready for them. He had already helped dig the cellar for the house, put up a barn for the animals, and arranged for a well to be dug. Then, leaning in on his elbows, he said, "Girls, you know this is a very serious move for us. The weather and crops are unknowns. Mama and I have talked and agreed that we will give this move a year. That said, we have faith in the founders of this village, and Mama and I will do everything we can to make our move a success and Egan our town."

Tuesday, May 18

As Papa directed the packing of the wagon, he kept out four bedrolls, the tripod, a large black kettle, and old tin plates and utensils for use on the road. These he piled at the back of the wagon just before he shut the tailgate. Mama put a basket of cold pork sandwiches for lunch and a crock of water with a wrapped piece of cooked beef chilled for the evening meal on the carriage floor.

Once the trunks and barrels had been stowed in the wagon, Papa and Mama lifted the black iron laundry pot and the cooking kettle and hung them on the side. The chickens clucked loudly and feathers flew as Papa fastened their coop to the wagon box and then tied their cow Bossy to the back.

Virgie, with tears swimming in her eyes, climbed into the carriage's backseat with Ruth, who reached over and patted her hand. "Papa said he would give Egan a year," she said. "So think of it as an adventure."

Virgie looked at her sister, who loved singing solos and doing readings. *Of course she thinks of this as an adventure,* thought Virgie. *Ruth makes friends wherever she goes. But I'm leaving Carrie and Catherine.*

Mama took the reins of the horses, Dusty and Pal. Papa cracked the whip over the heads of the oxen pulling the loaded wagon. "We are off to Egan!" Papa called.

Virgie turned around and took a last look at her neighborhood of modest frame houses interspersed with bare dirt fields. Someday the spindly cottonwood and ash saplings the families had planted around their houses would provide shade. On the hills to the northwest, she could see men building the large homes of those who had already made their fortune on the prairie. Virgie stood up in the carriage. "Goodbye, Carrie! Goodbye, Catherine!" she called out to the Carnahan twins and their mother, who stood waving on their front stoop.

The animals kicked up dust from the dirt road as the little caravan rolled north on Minnesota Avenue, jostling for space with other teams, carriages, and wagons that filled the road. Skinny dogs barked and yelped as they dodged the rolling wheels and the heavy plodding hooves of animals trying to keep their balance on the deep, sun-dried ruts.

Two thousand people now made Sioux Falls their home. *I'm going to miss this bustle*, thought Virgie. *I wonder how big it will be when we move back.*

She could hear the heavy breathing of the oxen as they pulled the loaded wagon up the steep Minnesota Avenue hill. She looked back at the canvas and wood shanties spread out on the treeless river flats. Newcomers would live there until they had the money to build a house.

At the top of the hill, Papa stopped the oxen and called out to Mama. "We're going to take the 'Indian Trail' to Republican and then Dell Rapids. Follow the wagon wheel tracks. I hope we can camp at Republican tonight. I would think we could make about four miles today."

The small caravan rattled and shuddered as it followed the sharp dips of the trail across the prairie. Virgie said, "We are really going slowly. I am going to be so bored."

Mama turned around and said, "Why don't you girls climb out and find some wild asparagus that we could cook for dinner. Don't go out of sight of either Papa or me."

"Come on," Ruth said. "Let's explore." The sisters ran across the prairie, the grasses not yet tall enough to drag on their skirts. "I see asparagus fern," Ruth called out. She and Virgie snapped off the stalks of new plants and put them in the wells of their aprons, which they held up.

"I didn't know asparagus was a prairie plant," Virgie said.

"I read that early pioneers planted asparagus to mark the graves of their loved ones who died on the trip west. And then it just spread," said Ruth.

The sun was high overhead. "Ah," Ruth said as they walked back to the carriage. "Breathe deeply. Smell the warming earth and sweet grass—a sure sign of summer."

"Wonderful," Mama said when she saw the stalks. "After lunch, look for wood for the fire tonight."

When they finally stopped by the river south of Republican, they began the nighttime ritual. Pa fed and watered the oxen and horses. Virgie took care of the chickens. Then she went over to the horses and rubbed their noses. "Good job, Pal. Good job, Dusty," she said as they nuzzled her neck.

Mama and the girls lifted out the tripod, untied the pot, found the dishes, laid out wood for the fire, hauled water from the river, and heated the water for the coffee. Pa put his bedroll under the wagon. With those supplies out of the wagon, there was room for Mama and the girls to shake the trail dust from their bedding and spread it on the wagon bed. Mama unwrapped the piece of cooked beef and scrubbed some potatoes to cook in the coals. "Wash the asparagus and then put it in this small pan," she said. "When the potatoes are almost done, we'll put the stalks over the fire for a few minutes and add some butter and salt."

It was not long after they had washed the final dish that the sun dropped below the horizon. "When the sun goes down, we go down. When the sun comes up, we are up," Pa said as he went to check on the horses one last time.

The rooster announced morning before the sun came up. Ruth milked Bossy while Mama cooked the oatmeal. Ruth skimmed off the cream and put it in a small wooden pail, tapped on the lid, and hung it from a hook under the wagon. "We'll see if this works," she said.

"I'll check for eggs," Virgie said as she unhooked the coop. She slid her hand under the hens and pulled out several smooth, warm eggs. She put them in a pot of water and they cooked while the family ate breakfast. They would be part of the lunch.

That evening as they unpacked their supplies, Ruth untied the small pail. "Mrs. Carnahan was right," she said as she opened the lid. "We have butter!" She would separate the butter from the whey that night at camp.

On day three, while washing breakfast dishes, Virgie was startled by the thud of the falling water keg and the clanging of the tin plates and cups. Papa was trying to store them in the wagon and they were falling to the ground.

"What's wrong, Papa?" asked Virgie.

"Nothing," he said.

Mama gave him a quick look and walked over to help pack the wagon.

"You and the carriage take the lead today," Papa said to Mama. "I'll follow behind."

"Virgie, you ride in the wagon with Papa. Ruth can be in the carriage," Mama said.

The small procession continued its journey. Later in the morning, Virgie was staring ahead at the trail. "I see something out there, but I can't tell what it is," she said to Papa.

"Where? I don't see anything," he said.

"Up there, farther on the trail. Oh, I see it now. It's a stagecoach! And it's traveling really fast." Virgie watched as Mama pulled her carriage off the trail to allow the stagecoach to pass. Papa kept his team on the trail.

Virgie could now see the flaring nostrils and the froth in the corners of the mouths of the lead horses as they strained to meet the demands of the stagecoach driver yelling out his commands. His face was frozen in a look of intense concentration as he worked to keep his team moving while not colliding with the slower wagon.

"Papa! Papa!" Virgie cried. "We have to move off the trail! Now!"

Papa flicked his whip over the oxen and they pulled over just in time.

Mama handed the horses' reins to Ruth, climbed out of the carriage, and hurried back to the wagon. "Ben, are your eyes watering again?" she asked in a worried voice.

"Yes," he said. "I was hoping they would clear up as the day went on, but they aren't. They are becoming worse. I can't see the trail."

"We need to change plans," said Mama kindly.

Virgie watched as her mother suddenly took charge. "Virgie, pour some water from the jug onto a towel and give it to your father. Ben, you ride in the carriage and rest with the towel over your eyes so they clear up. Ruth has handled the carriage in town, and I think she can handle it on the trail. I'll take the wagon and oxen. Virgie will ride with me."

Virgie and Mama climbed up on the wagon. "I've watched Papa for three days, so I think I can handle the oxen," Mama said as she flicked the whip over their heads. They started off.

"Will Papa be all right?" Virgie asked. "I was scared this morning when he couldn't see to tie on the pots and pans."

"Yes," Mama said. "I think he'll be better by tonight." When Papa was in the Confederate prison at Andersonville, Georgia, he had no shelter from the hot sun, the rain, or the damp cold weather, and doctors believed that caused the eye infection. It came and went. His eyes would become painful and water so badly that he had trouble seeing.

The next three days, they continued the new travel arrangements and were ready for the passing of the daily stagecoach.

"It must be going to Sioux Falls," Ruth said, "which means we can go back to visit."

Or even live there, thought Virgie. For now, at least she could send the letters she had been mentally writing to Carrie and Catherine.

Papa's eyes returned to normal that afternoon. During a quiet moment later in the day, he told Mama that in the back of his mind he was fearful there could come the day when his eyes would not return to normal. If that happened, how would he work and take care of the family? Mama said they would deal with it if it happened and not to worry about it now.

The seventh morning out, Papa said, "We'll stop in Dell Rapids today. There is a bridge where we can cross the river. We'll stay a day to rest the animals. I'll check over the wagon and carriage, buy any replacement parts, and pick up some more provisions."

The next morning, Mama said, "Let's find some fresh dandelion greens for dinner. They take about three hours to cook, and we have the time today." The three walked out among the large Sioux quartzite outcroppings that edged the prairie and the river at the dells and picked the greens.

The river splashed and gushed as it tumbled over the pink stone. Mama filled a pot with water, added the dandelion greens, and hung it over the fire. The girls dug worms and fastened them to the hooks on their poles and lowered them into a quiet, deep pool in a sharp curve of the river. They soon had fresh perch for dinner.

"Now we can rest until Papa returns," Mama said, stretching out on a quilt. The girls joined her. "Look up at the clouds," she said, squinting and peering skyward at the large, white puffs floating across. "When I was little, I would lie on my back and see images in the shapes of the clouds. What do you think they look like? I think I see a duck."

"I see a dog head above me," Virgie said.

"And a castle over there," Ruth said, pointing.

For the next hour, the three called out new images as the clouds shifted and moved on in the sky. "What good imaginations we have," Mama said as she stood up to start dinner.

As they ate, Papa told them Egan was fifteen miles away. It would take two days to reach Brookfield and then another day to Egan. The stores sold dried fruit and tins of vegetables, which he said he bought to supplement the wild greens, eggs, and fish they would eat until Egan stores had food supplies. "We are nearing the end of our journey," he said.

Thursday, May 27

The oxen snorted as they strained to go up the hill. At the top, Papa let them rest. Looking into the valley below, he said proudly, "There's our new home."

Virgie stood up and saw a gently rolling quilt of spring wildflowers and young green prairie grasses dotted with squares of newly turned black sod spread out before her. In front of the gentle hills to the east, trees outlined the Sioux River, which cradled the prairie. A dome of brilliant blue sky covered it all. *It's beautiful*, she thought.

"Where's the town?" she asked.

Papa pointed north. "There," he said.

Virgie looked, and in the distance she noticed a broad band where horses and wagons had trampled down the prairie grasses. Two narrower lanes intersected it. She counted two houses and three tents. *There is no town here*, she thought. *This is it? This is my new home?*

She felt sick to her stomach, just like the night she learned they were moving. She just knew this place was going to be boring. She could see no children playing. Where was the school? When could they move back to Sioux Falls? One year. One year. Isn't that what Papa had said? Tears filled her eyes as she thought of Carrie and Catherine.

Virgie sat back down in the carriage as they started down the hill and remembered Papa saying he had bought provisions to last until a store in Egan carried food supplies.

She could plainly see there was no store in Egan and certainly no provisions. *This is worse than I thought.*

Finally, the horses and oxen tired and sweaty, they stopped in front of one of the two houses. Virgie stared at the unpainted two-story frame house. The front was plain, and around the side she could see a small porch. The water well stood out in the grasses, directly opposite the side door. There was not a tree or bush nearby.

"Come on," Ruth said as she stepped down from the carriage. She grabbed Virgie's hand and pulled her toward the house. The two ran across the back porch and into the kitchen. A large pine table was in the middle of the room. A tall cupboard with open shelves was against the far wall.

Mama carried in a basket filled with household goods. "Papa worked hard to finish the table and cupboard and have the kitchen ready for us to move in," she said.

"Let's see where we are going to sleep," said Ruth.

The two ran up the stairs.

"Oh good, we do have our own bedrooms," Virgie said as she looked in the doorways of the three upstairs rooms.

Mama came up the stairs and said, "The next thing for you to explore is the barn, and you can do that by taking the chickens out to their new home. Ruth, you can take Bossy to the barn."

"Papa, did you really build the barn on your trip here?" Virgie asked as she carried the coop.

"Yes," he replied as he led the two horses out back. "I wanted to make sure the animals had shelter when we arrived. I also built the outhouse over there behind the house. That slanted door near the side porch leads down into the cellar where we can store our provisions.

"Now, I'll take care of the horses, and you can help Mama unload the wagon," he said.

Virgie and Ruth passed Mama carrying a box as they walked back to the wagon. "Let's see what we can do to make this house look like home," Mama said. "I want to finish before dark so we can go to the river and wash off. That dust from the trail is thick in my hair. And I'm hot."

Virgie was tired and dirty. Her happiness at having her own room was slowly eroding as she looked at the treeless land with two houses, no stores, no school—and no children. But washing off sounded good. So she joined the family in unloading the wagon. The four of them worked together to carry in the black iron stove and place it in a far corner of the kitchen.

Mama carefully unwrapped the Seth Thomas clock and placed it on a table in the parlor. "It made the trip in good shape," she said as she attached the pendulum. "Now, let's go to the river."

Mama quickly took some towels and soap out of a barrel, and they climbed back into the carriage and drove the half mile to the river. Papa went upstream. Mama and the girls removed their clothes, hung them on the nearby willows near the carriage, and entered the water.

"Oh," Virgie gasped as she waded into the cold water. She ducked beneath the surface and let the water run through her hair. "That feels delicious," she said when she came up. She scrubbed herself with the soap Mama had made with the oil of lavender, and the fragrance perfumed the water and the air. The scent lingered as they dressed and rode back home.

1880

June

Settlers Settle In

Tuesday, June 1

Virgie played impatiently with the ties of her sunbonnet as she stood outside the side door. "Hurry up!" she called. "We're going to miss it."

The door flew open and Ruth hurried out holding her bonnet in hand. "I'm ready," she said. The two girls ran down the grassy lane, their long skirts whipping about their legs. They crossed Third Street. "I can see it! Look!" Virgie cried.

There, seemingly floating above the prairie grasses, was a house. They saw a wagon under each corner of the house and two pairs of horses pulling each of the two forward wagons. The house swayed and lurched as the animals plodded over ruts that made up Roscoe Road. Riders on horseback were on either side of the house as it came up the lane to where the girls were standing. Up on the wagons, the one-and-a-half-story house towered over them and cast a big shadow. It shifted back and forth as the wagon wheels went over yet another bump.

"So that's how our house was moved from Roscoe," said Virgie. "I hope a family with girls moves into it. I'm tired of being the only children in town." Ruth nodded.

They jumped as a voice boomed behind them.

"Jack Latch and his family will be moving in there!" the voice announced. "And the general store will be moved this weekend."

The girls turned to see a beaming Charlie Mann, editor of *The Egan Express*. Mr. Mann had welcomed the Vandenbergs the day they arrived. Virgie silently wondered whether it was his chest puffed out with pride in the new town or his ample girth that threatened to pop the buttons on his vest. He was a big man with curly red hair and a droopy mustache.

He pointed to the right of the trampled grass that was now called Third Street. "That cellar is for the Roscoe House hotel. They have to cut the hotel in half to move it, but they'll have it here next week. A restaurant is planned for another building. Those men are repairing Latch's Hardware Store after its move. Then three houses from Roscoe will be placed on lots that were sold this week. Yes, you girls are lucky. You are seeing the birth of a town."

Virgie didn't think she was lucky. The two girls had learned quickly that Mr. Mann could talk on and on about the future of Egan.

At supper that night, Virgie looked around the house and thought about how her life had changed—and it did not make her feel better. The blue and yellow tablecloth and the white dinner plates should be on the table in Sioux Falls, not Egan. And the white lace curtains over the west window seemed to be mocking her as they fluttered happily in the breeze. Virgie wanted to be in Sioux Falls. But she was not. She thought she might be able to live with that for a year if she only had a friend.

Wednesday morning Virgie was doing the same chores she had done in Sioux Falls: feeding the chickens, gathering eggs, and skimming the cream off the milk for Ruth to make butter. She poured the milk into a tin container and lowered it by rope so it was just above the water level in the well. That kept the milk cool and fresh. Next up was gardening.

Mama directed Virgie and Ruth at work on what was to become their vegetable garden. Papa had done a rough plowing of the prairie sod, but the clods needed to be broken up into smaller pieces. "This dirt is so hard," Virgie said, whacking at a black piece of sod with a small shovel.

Finally, Mama said they would finish it the next

day and then plant the seeds and potato eyes she had brought from Sioux Falls. "We'll need potatoes, onions, carrots, and green beans," she said. "We have to plant them soon so the vegetables ripen before frost this fall."

That night over dinner, Papa told the family he would start his new job on Monday. "I need to make plans for the Cargill warehouse," he said. "I want to secure a prime location by the railroad tracks. The company has already ordered the lumber for the warehouse."

"Where will you find the grain for the warehouse?" asked Virgie.

"From the farmers who grow it," Papa said. "I'll spend time at the restaurant where I can visit with farmers who come into town to buy supplies. After I know where their homesteads are located, I'll take Dusty and ride out to meet with them."

Virgie used to like the family custom of telling the day's news at the dinner table, but not now. Papa turned to her and asked what her news was. "I don't have any news," she said with a pout. "My life is so boring. There are no girls my age. I have no one to play with. I want something interesting to happen."

Thursday morning, Mama woke the girls early to plant the garden before it rained. They finished the last row of carrots when the drops started falling.

The rain came in abundance. A late afternoon squall dropped egg-size hail on the prairie.

On a Saturday afternoon in late June, Mr. Mann, the newspaper editor, knocked on the door. "Hello, Virginia! Hello, Ruth!" he said. "School starts Monday. The school is still up by Roscoe. Hasn't been moved yet. Even so, I'd like to see you girls there."

The two girls ran up to their bedrooms and started pulling clothes out of their trunks.

Which one should I wear? Virgie wondered as she placed her indigo calico and her brown plaid on her round-top trunk. She stood back looking at her two dresses. She then shook out her best petticoat and pinafore and put them on the trunk. She would later take them downstairs to hang on the clothesline.

She looked around her small room. She decided to straighten it up so it would be ready for school.

The room had a narrow single bed along one wall, the round-top trunk, an oval rag rug, and a packing barrel holding her flannel undergarments, woolen leggings, and dresses. The top of the barrel was covered with a white lace doily her mother had made. On it sat a water pitcher, bowl, soap dish, toothbrush holder, and candleholder. Two hooks held her work dresses and undergarments.

On a shelf above the bed, she arranged the toy tea set and doll, gifts from her grandparents in Albert Lea, Minnesota,

when her family moved to
Dakota Territory. She
gently picked up the
small white porcelain
teapot and sat down
on her bed. She
carefully removed
the lid and took out
the paper on which
her grandparents had
signed their names. On
the back she made a tally mark. There

were now three marks, one for each week since they had
arrived in Egan. Papa had said one year. She would need
fifty-two marks. This would be her secret calendar.

She looked around her room. "It looks good," she said
as she flopped down on her pink and white quilt, soft from
many washings. She buried her face in it. "Oh, this smells
just like our house in Sioux Falls," she said. Her tears
flowed. Then she slept until suppertime.

When Papa walked into the house for supper, he said,
"Girls, look out that window. I don't like what I see. I
hope it doesn't hail. We were lucky that first hailstorm
didn't damage the house. I've put the horses and chickens
in the barn."

Virgie and Ruth pushed aside the white lace curtains
on the west kitchen window. "Oh, look at those clouds.

They're so dark they're purple," Virgie said.

"And look how they build towers in the sky," Ruth said. "I've never seen that before."

"Right," Papa said. "With no trees or buildings, it's a sweeping view to the horizon."

When they went to bed, the air was hot and quiet. Virgie quickly fell asleep. She was soon jolted awake.

She sat upright in bed. Thunder rolled and bellowed! It crashed and shook the house. Through her window she saw lightning jabbing the sky. The wind howled.

"Papa! Mama!" she cried as she jumped out of bed and ran to the hallway.

Ruth was already there. She grabbed Virgie's hand as they ran to their parents' bedroom. From its west window, they watched the lightning flashes light up heaven and earth.

"Look at that," said Papa in a low voice. "See that huge cloud straight ahead? And there's another one just like it to the north. They look like they're headed straight for town. Oh, no!" he cried as the clouds joined in a tumultuous mass and a tail dropped out and trailed down to earth.

"Run to the cellar!" Papa yelled. His shout jarred them from their almost hypnotic trance. They turned and ran down the stairs and out of the house. The wind hit with incredible force.

As soon as they stepped outside, tiny bits of debris hammered Virgie's face. The wind tore at her nightclothes. An even stronger blast hit. "Oh, it's going to blow me away!" she yelled. Ruth tightened her grasp on Virgie's hand.

They fought their way off the porch and to the cellar door. Papa struggled with the door, but he couldn't pull it open. "The wind's too strong!" he shouted. "Aggie, grab hold."

Together they pulled it open long enough for everyone to hurry down the steps. The door slammed behind them, and Papa pushed the bolt across the closing.

"Quick, under here," Mama said as she shoved Virgie under the cellar steps and up against the cold earthen wall. Shaking, Virgie sat against the wall, hunched into a ball. She was too scared to cry. Ruth crawled in next to her. Mama and Papa huddled on either side of the steps, their bodies forming barriers to protect the girls.

The screaming wind intensified into a shrieking fury. Whirling and roaring, the storm raged overhead. Virgie buried her head between her knees. The cellar door strained against the bolts and hinges as the wind wrenched it. The house shook, and dust filtered down from the cellar stairs above Virgie's head.

Suddenly it was over. Everything was quiet. No one said a word as they slowly crawled out from under the steps, unbolted the door, and climbed out of the cellar. The monstrous clouds were gone, and the world was still once again.

They looked around. Their house was still standing, and the shadowy outline of the barn was visible in the dark. "I'm glad I put the animals in the barn," Papa said.

Virgie dissolved into heaving sobs. "This place. I hate it. I don't want to live here. Do we have to wait a whole year? I want to go back to Sioux Falls now. It was safe there."

Papa knelt and wrapped her in his strong arms. "There, there," he murmured. "We're all safe." After she stopped sobbing, Papa said quietly, "We were lucky we had nothing like this in Sioux Falls, but tornadoes could happen there, too."

A block away, lanterns and torches flickered along Third Street, and voices came through the darkness.

"Are you better now, Virgie?" he asked, looking at her. She nodded tearfully. "Then let's go see how everyone else fared." Papa lit a lantern. Virgie kept a tight grip on his hand as the family walked toward Third Street. The path was littered with shredded lumber, leaves, and tree branches.

"Oh, no," Papa said as they reached Third Street. "Look at the buildings."

Down the street, the two-story hardware store had been lifted off its foundation and left in the empty lot next door. Barnard's General Store sat tilted against its foundation, as did Mrs. Cummings' Rooming House.

The Egan Express office teetered on its base. The half-finished blacksmith shop and stable lay in shreds.

"Look at the law office," Papa said. "It's in pieces. And the builder said it was the strongest structure in the village. Jackson's saloon is still standing in place."

"No, look," said Virgie. "The outside stairs are gone, and there's Dr. Detrick."

A small group of people had gathered in a circle under the door to the second-story living quarters of the saloon. The doctor was kneeling on the ground by the two little Jackson girls. Their mother, sobbing, sat next to them. Mr. Jackson, dazed, stood nearby.

The family approached Mr. Barnard, who saw the accident. He said he was looking out the door of his store when the storm hit. "I saw the Jacksons start down the outside stairway. Mrs. Jackson had just reached the ground when the storm swept the stairway away with Mr. Jackson and the girls still on it."

Mama gasped. "How awful. How are the girls?"

"Dr. Detrick says the four-year-old has a broken arm. The five-year-old is unconscious. He's still working on her," Mr. Barnard said. "Mr. Jackson's injuries aren't serious."

Mr. Barnard returned to the accident scene, and Virgie and her family turned to go home. As they did, Mr. Mann, with pencil and paper in hand, caught up to them. "I truly hope the Jacksons will be all right," he said. "But we can't let this discourage us. We have to rebuild. We've worked too hard getting this town started." Virgie saw nods of agreement from her parents.

When they got home, Virgie looked again at their house.

"I thought our house was sturdy and strong, but it looks very fragile now," she said to Ruth.

"Yes," Ruth answered. "It's really but a speck compared to this vast prairie."

When Virgie awoke in the morning, gentle breezes were brushing past the curtains, allowing sunbeams to pour into the room. She looked around at her things, all in place. *Last night doesn't seem real*, she thought as she dressed. She walked downstairs following the scent of ginger, cinnamon, and cloves coming from the kitchen.

"Where's Papa?" she asked.

"He got his tools from the barn and left early this morning to help repair the damage," Mama replied. "I'm going to take these ginger cookies to the men." She greased a cookie sheet with her muslin-wrapped stick.

Virgie sliced some bread and spread it with butter. She poured a glass of milk and sat down at the table. In the distance she could hear the sounds of men sawing wood and pounding with hammers.

"I want to help, too," said Virgie. "I could make sandwiches for them."

Mama nodded. "That would be nice," she said. "Do you want to grind up some meat?"

"No," said Virgie, getting up. "I'll make my favorite, brown sugar and butter."

"Well, maybe I'll add some smoked pork sandwiches, too," said Mama.

They worked together in silence as the stack of sandwiches grew. When they finished, Virgie placed the cookies and sandwiches in a basket and walked to Third Street.

"That's a welcome sight," said Papa, looking in the basket. "We're making good progress."

That afternoon, Virgie and Ruth hung their school dresses on the clothesline to air out.

At bedtime, Virgie was wide awake from the excitement of the storm and school. After she saw her parents' bedroom lamp go off, she tiptoed down to Ruth's room. "Are you awake?" Virgie whispered. She sat on Ruth's bed. "Last night was so scary. I thought I was going to be blown away. Weren't you frightened?" she asked, hugging her knees.

"Yes," Ruth admitted. "I felt safe in the cellar, but I was afraid the wind would blow away the house and we'd lose everything. We were so lucky. Are you nervous about starting school?"

"A little," Virgie said. "I don't know what the schoolhouse looks like, or the teacher."

They talked until nearly 11 p.m. How many students would be there? How old would they be? Would they be nice?

Monday, June 21

The girls awoke at 5:30 a.m. so they could finish their chores before leaving for school. Virgie gathered the eggs and weeded a couple of rows in the garden in the early morning light. Then she ran into the house, washed, and pulled on her indigo calico dress. She came downstairs to find that Mama had already packed cold pork sandwiches in their tin lunch pails and put on the lids.

Virgie sat down to a breakfast of eggs, bread, and milk. She picked at the food on her plate. Finally, she said, "Can I be excused? I can't eat this morning. I have butterflies in my stomach."

Mama nodded and said, "I understand."

The girls picked up their gray slates from the table and left for school. Mama joined them to see Roscoe and the school where the girls would be spending their days.

On the outskirts of town, they saw another girl walking with her mother. "Hello," they called out. The girl stopped and turned. She appeared to be about Ruth's age. Her mother nodded with a smile.

"Hi, I'm Mary DeBoer," said the girl. "We just moved here from Kansas. This is my ma, Mrs. DeBoer. Pa is opening a real estate office."

"Welcome to Egan," Mama said to the new friends. "We haven't been here much longer than you. There are lots of changes happening. How was your trip here? Were you able to take the train from Kansas City to Sioux City?"

"Please, call me Louise," Mrs. DeBoer said as she and Mama continued walking toward Roscoe, exchanging news about the dance social to be held at the schoolhouse that Friday night.

Mary, Ruth, and Virgie ran ahead past the empty cellars and bare dirt spots where buildings had once stood. "Pa was here when the first houses were being moved from Roscoe," Mary said as they slowed to a walk. "He liked what he saw and came back to Kansas to bring us here." Not even two dozen houses and stores remained between patches of overgrown grasses and a few skinny trees. The shouts of two boys chasing each other in and around the open foundations brought them to a stop.

"Oh, dear," Ruth said. "Look at those empty cellars. Those boys shouldn't be near them. Who are they? The walls could collapse and they could get hurt. Virgie, don't you walk near those openings," she said. Virgie nodded.

The girls walked past the school bell, in its frame atop a post, near the front door. The two wooden outhouses, boys' on the left and girls' on the right, were in back.

"That must be our teacher," Virgie said as she looked at the man standing by the front door of the school. He was of medium height and weight, about thirty-five years old. He wore wire-rimmed glasses, and his brown hair was thinning above his forehead.

"Hello, I'm Mr. Nelson," he said as he greeted the young scholars at the door. Virgie quickly counted fifteen children, with Ruth and Mary among the oldest. When Mr. Nelson came into the classroom, he started assigning seats. "Normally, I assign two students to a desk, but since there are more than enough places for everyone, I'll give each older student a desk." Ruth and Mary each got one in the back of the room.

"Virgie," Mr. Nelson said, "I'm going to give you a desk by yourself but expect to have a seatmate as more people move into Egan." She nodded as she slid behind the flat-topped desk.

Virgie recognized the two boys who had been running around the empty cellars. Mr. Nelson identified them as Danny and Joey Thompson and seated them in front of Virgie.

Danny turned around and whispered loudly to Virgie, "You have a dumb name. Who gave you that?"

Virgie blushed. "My parents gave me the name," she said defensively. "It's short for Virginia." She scowled. *Could my life be any worse?* she thought. *No town, no girls my age, no friends, and now a mean boy right in front of me. No one has ever said my name was dumb.* She was relieved to hear Mr. Nelson start talking to the class.

"We will first learn a little about each other," Mr. Nelson said. "I know some of you come several miles from claims out on the prairie. Some of you walk the two miles from Egan. Tell the class where you live, what you like to do, and a little about your family."

Virgie admired Ruth's poise and confidence as she stood up front and told of her interest in music and the singing and readings she had done at holiday observances and church services in Sioux Falls.

When Ruth sat down, Danny turned around again and said, "She isn't really your sister, is she? You don't look at all alike."

"Danny," Mr. Nelson said. "Do you have something important to share with the class?"

Danny shook his head and slouched down at his desk.

Virgie thought what a rude and unlikeable boy he was. Her stomach turned. She was confused by Danny's comments and trying to think of what she would say.

When Mr. Nelson called "Virginia Vandenberg," she wiped her sweaty palms on her skirt and stood up. "Ruth is my sister. We live one block south of Third Street in a house moved from Roscoe. Papa is the grain buyer." She could see Danny making faces at her. But she continued, "My favorite book, err, color is light blue. My favorite subject is reading, but I also love music. And I like to draw and paint. I don't like spiders. This winter Mama is going to teach me to make lace, if I master my sewing stitches." With relief she sat down. She was mad at herself for being distracted by Danny. *That's not going to happen again*, she thought.

Danny turned around again and whispered, "So you don't like spiders. And you're skinny. I'm going to call you 'Spider.'" He turned back as Mr. Nelson went to the front of the class. Then it was Danny's turn.

Danny shoved his hands down into his pants pockets and said, "We're from Illinois but moved first to a farm in Iowa. When Pa heard of new land in the west being opened, he decided to pack us up again and move us up here. He has a claim across the river and about a mile south of Egan. He's planting it in wheat. Me and Joey don't have any other brothers or sisters."

After all the students had their turn, Mr. Nelson told them about himself. He not only taught school, but he had also staked a claim on 160 acres of prairie one-half mile west of the schoolhouse. "I needed two three-horse teams to plow 46 acres of that prairie sod, and I planted it in sugar cane. If I keep improving the land and living there, I'll own it in four more years," he said. "My hobbies are playing the tuba and singing. I met my wife at church, where she played the organ. I will include music in our lessons.

"Now," he said, "I have a local history question to ask you. Why was Egan named Egan?"

Mary raised her hand. "My father told me the town was named after Mr. J.M. Egan, who is the superintendent of the Southern Minnesota and Milwaukee Company Railroad."

"That's correct, Mary," said Mr. Nelson.

Virgie was glad she sat on the east side of the room where the morning sun poured in. Behind her desk was a corner cloakroom with hooks on the wall for coats. Notches along the door frame held a wooden exercise bar. In the other corner was a stack of wood piled behind a large potbellied stove. Up front, a picture of President George Washington hung to the left above the chalkboard, and one of President Abraham Lincoln hung to the right. Virgie felt right at home in a schoolroom.

That night Virgie sat down to supper and said, "I've got news to tell. Mr. Nelson is our teacher, and he has a claim. He is growing sugar cane, not wheat. I have a desk to myself for now. And there are two horrid boys sitting in front of me. They made me stumble in my speech about myself. Tell me again, why was I named Virgie?" she asked.

"Because," Mama said, "I had a wonderful mother whose name was Virginia, and we honored her by giving you her name. Be proud of it."

Mama had news also. "The mothers on the walk back to Egan talked about the dance social at the schoolhouse this weekend. Sounds like fun."

Ruth said she had heard that the little Jackson girl who had been hurt in the tornado had regained consciousness.

"We started work on the site for the grain warehouse," Papa said. "The Cargill and Van warehouse will be thirty by eighty feet, the largest in Egan. And the railroad crew plans to grade a sidetrack on the east side of the main track to accommodate all of the wheat farmers and lumber men. It'll be good for my business."

Friday, June 25
Mama said she was going to set an early table that night because she and Papa were going to the dance social at the schoolhouse. "We should have a good time. We haven't had time to do much socializing. Almost everyone in town is going. You girls will be fine here by yourselves."

"This has been an exciting week," said Papa at supper. "I heard that forty new people moved into town. They're getting off of every stagecoach and staying at the hotel. Did you see all the tents and canvas-covered wagons around town?"

"I saw people walking around Roscoe," Ruth said. "Are they buying houses to move to Egan?"

Papa nodded.

"But there are still no girls my age," Virgie moaned.

"You're right," Papa said. "But I'm sure there will be. I talked to a number of men who are looking at possible opportunities. After they find space for their businesses, they'll go back to Wisconsin or Kansas and bring their families. Like Mary's father. Maybe a family with children will move into the house across the field."

After dinner, Mama unfolded her best calico dress from the trunk and slipped it over her head. The cream-colored background of the fabric and the collar's soft lace folds contrasted nicely with her dark hair.

When she came downstairs, Virgie said, "You look beautiful, Mama."

"Let's go, Aggie girl," called Papa as he finished hitching the horses to the carriage. Virgie and Ruth waved as the carriage headed down the lane.

Ruth was reading and Virgie had nodded off in a chair in the parlor when their parents returned from the dance. "How was it?" Ruth asked. "Who played the music? Who else was there? Is the schoolhouse big enough for a dance?"

Mama said most of the couples in the village were there as well as some who lived on nearby claims, and they filled up the schoolhouse.

"The musicians came up from Dell Rapids," Papa said. "I wouldn't mind dusting off my trumpet and joining a group some night. Hearing that music made me want to play again."

Early Sunday evening, the Vandenbergs joined other families at Egan's first religious service. They climbed the outside stairs to the second floor of Latch's Hardware Store. Crates and empty boxes were set up for seating on the wooden floor of the large room.

"There are four empty crates by those east windows," said Papa as they walked across the room.

"I can hardly see the front," said Virgie as she stretched her neck. "Is that the minister standing next to the barrel?"

"Yes," Mama said. "He'll be coming the six miles from Flandreau when we have services."

The room was warm and stuffy, but Virgie could feel cool puffs of fresh evening air come through the open windows. Even so, she found it hard to stay awake during the hour-long sermon.

Her mind drifted. Almost everything in her life had changed in the past four weeks, and it wasn't for the better, she was sure. The minister had just placed the Bible next to the glass jar of wildflowers on top of the barrel. It certainly wasn't like the church in Sioux Falls, where two vases of garden flowers would have decorated that altar. That church was not big, but it had a tall, white steeple and arched gothic windows. The sun would filter through the glass of the south-facing window, casting the oak altar, the brass cross, and the assembled congregation in a soft, beautiful light. Her schoolmates, neighbors, teachers, and friends would have been sitting there. *That light wrapped us all in a mantle of warmth. I felt so loved and protected,* thought Virgie.

A cough interrupted her musing and brought her back to the plain, bare second-story room of the hardware store.

Why did we have to move? she thought. *Papa had a fine job in Sioux Falls. We had a nice house. I lived close to school and had friends who lived just at the end of the block.*

Virgie heard the minister talk about blessings. *What blessings do I have?* she asked herself. Danny certainly wasn't a blessing and never would be, she was sure. The new house wasn't painted, and she didn't want to count that as a blessing. They didn't live in a town, just a cluster of buildings with people moving in and out and in and out. There was not even a confectionary shop where they could buy candies on their way home from church, as was their custom in Sioux Falls.

But then there were her parents. *They are definitely a blessing,* she thought. It was a blessing that Papa's eye infection had not returned, so he could work at his new job. Ruth was well, and the consumption she had two years ago had not returned. *Maybe,* thought Virgie, *my life does have some blessings.*

She stood with her parents as the minister asked them to sing "Amazing Grace." The voices blended together and swelled as the congregation brought forth the old hymn's familiar words.

As the Vandenbergs walked home in the dusk, Virgie said to her mother, "That didn't seem like church. It's just a big room, nothing like Sioux Falls. Then I heard the minister talk about blessings, and I thought about my blessings. I do have some blessings, and I am thankful."

Mama took her hand and gave it a squeeze. "I know," she said quietly.

Monday, June 28

After school Virgie had just finished dropping ginger cookie dough onto the baking sheets when she saw a loaded wagon and oxen in front of the house across the field.

"Can I go over? Please?" she begged Mama. Mama nodded, and Virgie was off.

She picked her way across the grassy field until she neared the house. Then she stopped. She looked. What if there were no children? She watched quietly as two men and a woman carried in boxes and rolled in large packing barrels. After a few minutes, from around the corner of the house came a little boy, about three years old, followed by another, just a toddler.

"Wait a minute," came a girl's voice. "You can't go around there. You'll be in the way."

Virgie saw a girl who looked to be ten or eleven years old run around the corner and grab the children's hands. She had blond hair woven in braids and wore a green-and-white gingham dress with a white apron.

Virgie started walking. She felt a knot in her stomach. What if the girl didn't want to be friends? Still, Virgie thought, she had to try. She stepped closer and called out, "Hello." The new neighbor looked up.

"Hello," Virgie said again. "Are you the new family? My name is Virgie Vandenberg. I live over there," she said, pointing to the house across the field.

The blond girl, holding each boy's hand tightly in hers, walked across the yard.

"Hello, Virgie," she said. A bright smile lit up her face. "Yes, we just moved here from Faribault, Minnesota—my name is Lottie Latch. These are my brothers, Eddie and Willis. Willis is the baby. My pa moved the hardware store from Roscoe, and he'll open it in a couple of weeks."

"Do you want to play?" asked Virgie.

"I can play tomorrow after school," Lottie said. "Is the school really two miles away?"

"Yes," answered Virgie. "Do you want to walk with my sister and me in the morning?"

They walked to school together the next morning, and after they walked home that afternoon they stood in front of Latch's Hardware Store and watched as teams of horses pulled four wagons, each carrying one corner of one half of the two-story Roscoe House hotel. They moved slowly down the road and placed it on its Third Street lot. "I can't believe how quickly the village is growing," Virgie said. "When we arrived there were two houses: one for the newspaper editor and his office, and one for us. Just this month they have added your house, a general store, a restaurant and bakery, Mrs. Cummings' Rooming House, your father's hardware store, and now the hotel."

Lottie looked at the few frame structures. "Living on the prairie is going to take getting used to. It's different. Even the buildings. In Faribault, they were built of limestone, not wood like here. But Pa is excited about his new store. I am glad we moved here."

Wednesday after school, Virgie and Lottie helped unpack the crates and barrels at Barnard & Lowe & Co.'s General Store. Lottie's father was still waiting for his hardware store supplies to arrive, so the two girls were free to help others. Mr. Barnard quickly enlisted their assistance. "It's almost like Christmas and opening gifts," said Lottie as they started on another barrel.

"Oh, I am so glad they sell these," said Virgie, holding up glass jars of cinnamon sticks and candied lemon and orange peels. "Mama makes a delicious pudding with lemon and cinnamon."

Virgie and Lottie cooed over the Barnards' baby, Grace, as she stretched and kicked in her cradle in the store. "She is so cute," said Virgie as Grace's small hand encircled Virgie's little finger.

As they walked out of the store, Virgie said, "That

was fun being the first to see the new things the store is going to sell. I've never done anything like that before. Maybe, if there is nothing else happening, we can do it again tomorrow."

1880

July

Living the History

Friday, July 2

Several times on the walk to school that morning, the four girls had to step off the road and walk around oxen pulling heavily loaded wagons.

"Did you see all the wagons on the road?" Virgie asked Mr. Nelson as she walked in the door.

"Yes, I've been watching them since I opened up school this morning," he replied. "So far, I've counted fifteen wagons. If this keeps up, it's going to be hard to concentrate on our studies." With the railroads pushing the tracks farther west and the Homestead Act offering free land, settlers were pouring into the territory.

Sitting at their desks, the students watched out the windows and found many excuses to leave their desks so they could walk next to the window and wave and smile at the settlers in what seemed to be a never-ending procession of wagons, carts, oxen, and horses, all heading west. Furniture, household goods, lumber, chicken coops, barrels, trunks, and children took up every inch of space on the wagons. Cows walked behind. Cries of babies, the lowing of cattle, the shouts of the wagon drivers, the neighing of horses, the squeaking of wagon wheels, and the creaking of lumber rubbing against wooden containers all combined to announce the arrival of the settlers. They waved and smiled at the faces in the schoolhouse window.

During the lunch break, the students lined the road, waving and talking to the settlers as they passed by. The children called out, "Hello!" "Hello!" "Where are you from?"

The travelers, waving back, answered, "Wisconsin." "Illinois." "Minnesota." "Kansas."

"Where are you going?"

"West, out west."

Virgie and Lottie saw a girl about their age walking alongside a wagon nearing the school. "Let's go talk to her," said Virgie.

The two ran to the side of the road where she was walking. "Hello. Where are you from?" Virgie asked.

"Hello," the girl responded, smiling. But that was all Virgie and Lottie could understand. Everything else she said was in a language they didn't know.

"Oh," said Virgie, waving goodbye as they walked back

into the schoolhouse. "I wish we could have talked to her. I wonder where she was from."

Mr. Nelson overheard them and said the immigrants heading west were from many countries: Norway, Sweden, Great Britain, Ireland, Germany, and Russia. After lunch, the trail became drier, and billows of dust were kicked up with every hoof step and turn of the wagon wheel until the procession was wrapped in a brown cloud.

"Can we please close the windows?" asked Ruth, sneezing. Mr. Nelson nodded and helped the students shut the windows.

Some of the students had been counting the wagons and carts passing through town, and by the end of the school day they had tallied more than one hundred of them going west.

"This is a remarkable day," Mr. Nelson said. "You are watching history in the making, the westward expansion of this country. In fact, you're living it, just by being in Dakota Territory."

At supper, the girls told their news. "Can you believe it? One hundred wagons," said Virgie.

"I had no idea there were that many," Papa said. "My news is that I sold our oxen and wagon to one of those families. They were from Wisconsin and needed a bigger and stronger team. That was a good sale. They paid me $125 for the team and wagon, $25 more than I paid for it. I picked up a smaller cart for hauling supplies at a good price from another family. Now we have money to buy supplies, and I won't have to feed the oxen over the winter."

"How can there be enough land for everyone?" Ruth asked.

"The territory is huge. Thousands and thousands of acres," said Papa. "But I'd want to be one of these early settlers so I could claim the best farmland. Roscoe Road is just one of the trails going west. I saw Mr. Mann this morning. He said so many people are moving into Dakota that there is talk of the territory becoming a state."

Papa opened up the pages of *The Egan Express*. "There is some great news for Egan in the paper this week," he said. "'A. Burd bought an 80-acre tract of land between the town plat and the river. It contains quite a body of timber, which Mr. Burd proposed to protect on account of the beauty it lends to the town. A praiseworthy purpose.'" Papa put down the paper. "That will be a great place to picnic with all those shade trees. We need to thank Mr. Burd when we see him."

Mama said, "I have additional news to share. The post office has moved from Roscoe to Barnard's store. Oh, I forgot," she said, standing up and going into the parlor. She returned, carrying an envelope. "This is for you, Virgie. From the Carnahans."

Virgie quickly opened it and read. Then she looked up.

"Carrie and Catherine are so disappointed. A family with four boys moved into our old house." Virgie picked up the letter again and said, "Oh, the twins have a new hairstyle. Their mother cut their hair, and they both have bangs now. And they're having a Fourth of July picnic."

"Mama, could Ruth cut my hair into bangs and keep the front short? It would be easier to comb," Virgie said.

"Are you sure you want to cut your hair?" Mama asked. "It is so pretty when we wrap your long hair to create curls."

"Yes, I want it cut," Virgie said. "It's hard to sleep with my hair rolled around those rags."

"All right," Mama said, "if Ruth will do it."

Then Virgie said wistfully, "I loved the Fourth of July parade in Sioux Falls. At school I hear talk of celebrations in Pipestone and Flandreau. Why can't we have one here?"

"As Mr. Mann said in the paper, we're too busy building a town. We don't have time," Mama said. "But don't fret. I'm sure we will do something special that day."

Virgie spent the next day wondering what that something special could be.

Sunday, July 4

The girls awakened the morning of July 4 to find Mama already working in the kitchen.

"Gather your things," she said. "We're going to the river for a picnic with Lottie's family."

They loaded up the carriage with old patchwork quilts. Mama packed roasted chicken, potato salad, bread, carrots, and sugar cookies into baskets.

"Are you bringing enough for everyone?" asked Virgie, watching in amazement at the amount of food going in the baskets.

"Yes," Mama said. "Mrs. Latch isn't feeling strong, so I offered to bring the meal for all of us." They drove over to the Latch house, and soon the little parade of two carriages headed east to the Sioux River for an Independence Day celebration. Papa pulled into a leafy grove of burr oak and cottonwood trees.

They spread the quilts and set the hampers down. Mama said, "Here, Ruth, would you please set this jar of lemonade in a shady shallow curve of the river? It will keep it chilled."

Virgie and Lottie watched Lottie's father help Eddie bait the hook of his bamboo pole with a worm and throw it into the water. It didn't take long before Eddie caught several small perch. The girls explored the riverbanks and found a plum thicket, the branches filled with tiny fruit. They would come back and pick ripe plums to make jelly and syrup for winter.

Up over the banks they climbed and ran out onto the prairie. "Oh, the flowers!" Virgie cried. "The world is in bloom." With shouts of delight the girls gathered armloads of pink prairie coneflowers, purple prairie clover, and white meadow anemones, which they presented to their mothers. Mama emptied the carrots out of a jar onto a plate, filled the jar with river water, and arranged the wildflowers. She placed it in the center of the quilt and then the food around it. "That looks so pretty, Mama," Virgie said.

After lunch, everyone rested on the quilts and talked of other Fourth of July celebrations. Virgie knew this holiday was important to Papa. He had fought in the Civil War and had been captured and imprisoned by the Confederacy.

"Yes," he said. "You children should be proud of this country and that it is celebrating 104 years as a nation." He pulled from his pocket, as was his Independence Day custom, a tattered copy of the song "Tramp, Tramp, Tramp." He paused and stroked the downward curl at the end of his mustache. Then he solemnly read one of the stanzas to the two families.

"So within the prison cell we are waiting for the day
That shall come to open wide the iron door;
And the hollow eye grows bright, and the poor heart
    almost gay
As we think of seeing home and friends once more."

Virgie heard Papa's voice choke up as he finished the prisoner's lament.

The sun grew hotter, and soon the children were ready for a dip in the river. Just upstream from the picnic site flowed a small series of rapids, but then the Sioux River spread out into a calm stretch. The two fathers stretched out on the quilts for a snooze. Before placing his hat over his face, Papa warned the children, "The river is running full after all that rain, so be careful and stay in the shallows by the sand bar. The main channel has deep holes and dangerous currents."

Mama, Mrs. Latch, and the girls pulled up their skirts and went wading. The boys played and splashed in the shallow water near shore and built little dams with the muddy sand. While Ruth and the two mothers stood near the little boys and visited, Virgie and Lottie waded in the cool water, laughing and giggling as the mud squished up between their toes. They were talking when they were distracted by the noise of an animal in the bushes on the opposite bank. Virgie, intent upon seeing what kind of animal it was, walked farther out into the river.

Suddenly, her footing gave way and she fell into a hole in the river. "Help!" she yelled just before she sank below the surface of the river. Kicking her legs and thrashing her arms, she rose to the surface as the current seized her. She heard everyone yelling as she struggled to keep her head above water. She knew the current was carrying her farther and farther away from her family and could feel her wet skirt and petticoat pulling her down in the water.

"The tree! The tree!" she heard her mother shouting. Just ahead, she spotted a tree that had fallen into the river. The current brought her within reach of the smallest branches, and she grabbed one, struggling to hold on as the water fought to tear her away. Her father, awakened by the shouting, ran across the field and out onto the tree trunk. He was soon lifting her out of the river.

Papa hugged his soaking daughter. Then he held her at arm's length and, looking solemnly into her face, said, "Did I not say 'Stay in the shallows?'"

Virgie, still shaking with fright, nodded her head. Between her chattering teeth, she said, "I'm sorry. I didn't mean to. I just wanted to see the animal on the other bank."

Papa gave her another hug. Mama ran up and wrapped a quilt around her shivering daughter.

Virgie sat quietly on the carriage ride home. No one spoke.

Thursday, July 8

At school, the students talked of a circus coming to the nearby town of Flandreau. Virgie thought it sounded like fun. As she and Lottie walked home from school that afternoon, they ran into Mr. Mann on the road.

"Hello, Mr. Mann," Virgie said. "Are you going to write about the circus coming to Flandreau?"

"Ahhhh, the circus," he replied, and his smile disappeared. "Let me caution you girls. It's Monty Miles's show, a one-horse operation. It'll probably take away a good many dollars that might be better spent. I wouldn't recommend it."

As the girls continued on their way, Virgie said, "I still think the circus sounds like fun."

When she got home, she helped Mama shell the fresh peas she had bought at Barnard's. After cooking some for supper, they would dry most of them for eating during the winter.

"Did you know a circus is coming to town?" Virgie asked.

Mama nodded. "People at the store say it's not a very good circus. Papa and I will discuss it."

At that moment Papa came in the door. "Good. Fresh peas for dinner. My favorite," he said, grabbing a small handful and popping them in his mouth. "Did you see the new ash and butternut trees the Barnards planted? We should plant some so we'll have some shade."

"Did you see their sweet baby Grace?" Virgie asked. "I hope they will let me come over and play with her sometime." Papa said she was in the house sleeping, so he had not.

When Virgie and Ruth saw Mr. Mann the next day, he told them he and his wife had finally moved from the back of the printing shop into their own house. "Look how the town has come back," he exclaimed. "There are no signs of the tornado. Four more houses were moved last week, and others are coming. Did you know Egan is the geographic center of Moody County? We'll be the future metropolis of Moody County.

"Look at this," he added, pulling a copy of the *Chicago Times* from his inside pocket. "I've been showing this to everyone." He opened the paper and read, "'The Territory of Dakota, with an area double that of England and fully as large as France . . .'" He stopped. "'Fully as large as France.' Did you hear that?" he asked.

Virgie nodded. She thought living in a territory as large as France was very impressive.

He continued, "'The Territory of Dakota, with an area double that of England and fully as large as France, is capable of supporting millions of people. Rain falls in abundance during the growing season, but little snow in the winter. Corn grows well but wheat will become the product of this territory, as it is most profitable. Although this region is necessarily young, thriving towns containing churches, schools, enterprising newspapers, and nearly every advantage are to be found on every hand.'"

He paused for a breath, beamed, and said, "That is us. Do you know that nearly a carload of this edition of the *Times* was shipped to Europe? More and more people will move here." Mr. Mann tucked the paper into his pocket and continued down the street.

A clap of thunder startled them. "Sounds like rain," Ruth said. "Let's head home." And they started running down the lane.

Wednesday, July 14

On their walk to school early the next week, Virgie and Lottie could see men haying their fields. They watched a settler swing the long, curved blade of his scythe across the stems of the tall prairie grasses.

"Look! A kitten," said Virgie, pointing to a calico ball of fluff pouncing on the fallen grasses.

"Is that your kitten?" she asked the settler.

"Nope," he replied. "Probably a stray."

Virgie turned to Lottie. "Let's catch him and take him home."

Lottie shook her head. "We don't have time. We'll be late for school."

"No, we won't. Come on," said Virgie as she started running across the field. She chased the kitten into the nearly five-foot-tall big bluestem grasses, concentrating on keeping him in sight. Lottie was right behind her. Suddenly, Virgie couldn't see him. "Where did he go? Do you see him?" she asked. Lottie shook her head. Virgie ran this way then that, searching for him. Finally, she said, "I guess we won't find him now. We'd better go to school." She turned around and could see nothing but the tall grasses surrounding them. "Oh, no," she said, "which way is Roscoe Road?"

Virgie and Lottie looked around. They had run back and forth so many times searching for the kitten that bent grasses were going in all directions. They took a few steps one way, then another. "This isn't working," Lottie said. "Let's stop and talk about how we can find our way out."

The two stood still and tried to decide which way to go. "Wait a minute," Virgie said. "When we sit at our desks in the morning, the sun shines on us from the east windows. I can feel the sun on my bonnet. That direction is east. School is north of us. We came in from the west so we need to walk that way, with the sun hitting our backs."

The girls started walking west and in a couple of minutes found grasses bent over where they had walked earlier. Soon, they were out on the cut field and running toward school.

The school door creaked as they slowly opened it. Virgie felt thirteen pairs of eyes on her. "What is that grass sticking to your skirt?" asked Ruth in a loud whisper.

"Please take your seats," Mr. Nelson said. "We're in the middle of a lesson. I'll talk to you both later." The girls slid behind their desk, got out their primers, and started reading.

Later that morning, a shadow fell across Virgie's book. She looked up to see Mr. Nelson standing over them. "Virginia, why were you girls almost an hour late for school?" he asked.

"It's my fault," Virgie said. "Lottie told me not to chase the kitten, but I wanted to take it home so badly. Then we got lost in the prairie grasses. I'm really sorry. We won't be late again."

Mr. Nelson said, "You know, you were lucky to find your way out. Those big bluestem and Indian grasses can be six feet tall and thick. Children have been known to get lost for good in them. You need to stay out of them."

Mr. Nelson said they were to eat lunch at their desks and not play over the noon hour. They could study spelling and arithmetic to make up the time missed.

Virgie read the first two problems:

1. A man bought a sleigh for $142, a carriage for $325, and a pair of horses for $476. What was the cost of all?

2. Dakota contains 147,700 square miles. Massachusetts 8,040. How many states as large as Massachusetts can be made out of Dakota, and how many square miles will be left over?

After school, Ruth was waiting for Virgie and Lottie. "What happened?" she asked. "Where did you catch grass in your skirt? Why were you girls so late?"

Virgie once again told her story.

"Mama's not going to be happy," said Ruth. Virgie already knew that.

After hearing Virgie's story, Mama repeated Mr. Nelson's warning about the danger of the tall prairie grasses. She added cleaning out Bossy's stall in the barn to Virgie's weekly chore list.

When Papa walked in the door that night, he was smiling and excited. "This is going to be a great fall," he said. "The railroad track is just a week from Egan and the railroad bridge is almost done. When the track is finished, I'll ship in lumber to build my warehouse. Farmers coming into town are all predicting bumper wheat and corn crops. They know I'm the buyer for

Cargill and Van, and I've told them to expect to see me at their place in the next few weeks with contracts for their grain. Mr. Barnard and Mr. Latch tell me business is so good they're ordering new merchandise for their stores."

Virgie asked, "Was there mail today?" She was hoping for a letter from Carrie and Catherine.

"No. The stages still can't cross the river with the water so high from all the rain," Papa said. "That's a problem. We have to build a bridge over the Sioux River before harvest. It would be too dangerous for wagons loaded with wheat and corn to cross the river the way it is now."

Wednesday, July 21

"The railroad bridge is completed!" Papa announced as he walked in the door after work. "The track reaches Egan tomorrow. The first train arrives Friday. The lumber for my warehouse is on its way." Work on his warehouse would start Saturday, and it would be ready for business in two weeks.

On Friday afternoon, Virgie walked with her family to the railroad track and joined most of the other villagers leaning over and peering east down the track. Soon they saw the big black steam engine with two columns curling upward into the sky—a white one of steam and a dark gray one of smoke. The acrid smell of the burning coal filled the air. The brakes caught on the steel wheels with a screech. The people clapped and cheered for the train's arrival.

Virgie overheard snippets of conversation as she walked among the crowd.

"I'll be ordering more lumber to add on to my store. . . ."

"I'm sending in an order to double our inventory of boots and shoes. . . ."

"My cousin in Minnesota is looking for a place to open her bakery, and this is it. . . ."

"With the train, we can go back to Minnesota and see my parents. . . ."

Maybe I could go live with my cousins in Albert Lea or visit the twins back in Sioux Falls, Virgie thought.

That Saturday morning, Virgie woke up early to clean out Bossy's stall. "This is not fun. Yuck, it's stinky," she said to Bossy as she filled up the wheelbarrow with old straw and cow pies and took them out to the manure pile. After spreading clean, fresh straw, Virgie stood back and said, "There, Bossy. Your home is clean."

As she left the barn, Papa walked up to her. "I know winter is a long way off, but I have been thinking about our preparations for it," he said. "When we clean Bossy's stall, we need to shovel the cow pies and place them along the edge of the field behind the barn so the sun can dry them. The same with horse droppings. Then we'll stack them. If we have to, we can burn them for fuel this winter. That's why they call it 'prairie coal.'"

Virgie wrinkled her nose. They would be burning cow pies? She had never heard of that. *Would it be smelly? It doesn't sound very appetizing*, she thought. *We'd never have to do that back in Sioux Falls.*

Early Monday morning, Virgie finished her chores, went into the house, washed, changed clothes, and waited for Lottie so they could walk to school.

When Virgie answered the door, she could see Lottie had been crying.

"What's wrong?" asked Virgie.

"The Barnards' baby Grace died of diphtheria last night. Mrs. Barnard and their little boy have it, too," Lottie said.

Virgie gasped. Diphtheria here in Egan? It was a very contagious disease that caused a high fever and made it hard to breathe. Last week she had heard her parents talk of two young children in neighboring villages dying from it. But baby Grace? Virgie had just played with her at the store. She ran to tell her mother. It didn't seem possible that little Grace was dead.

"Oh, I didn't know," Mama said sadly. "And I just heard that Dr. Detrick's baby has taken a turn for the worse."

Neither Virgie nor Lottie talked as they walked to school; each was lost in her own thoughts.

That week, their parents attended funerals for the Barnard and Detrick babies. The good news was that Mrs. Barnard and her son were feeling better.

1880

August

Big Changes Coming Soon

Saturday, August 7

For several days, Virgie wondered how she could persuade her parents to let her go to the circus. Finally, during one hot, smelly day cleaning the stalls, the idea came. She talked to Papa. "If I cleaned Bossy's stall for another week, would you please give me money to go to the circus?" Her parents agreed that she could go that Saturday with Lottie, Eddie, and their father. Mrs. Latch would stay home with Willis.

"I still don't think this is a good idea," said Mama as she counted out the coins for Virgie's admission. "Remember Mr. Mann's warning about the kind of circus Monty Miles puts on? I think it's going to be a waste of good money."

"No, it won't," Virgie said. "I know it's going to be fun. You'll see. Thank you for letting me go." She gave

Mama a hug and ran out the door. She climbed into the back seat of the carriage with Lottie and Eddie. Mr. Latch was at the reins.

Mr. Latch followed the crowd to Flandreau and down a path to the circus tent where a clown directed them to an area where they could leave their carriages and horses. Then they headed to the tent.

"The tent looks like it has sails. See how the sides billow in and out with the wind," said Virgie. Mr. Latch bought the tickets for them. As they walked through the tent flap, Virgie could hear a small band playing to one side. She sniffed the air. "It kind of smells like freshly cut wood at the lumber yard. But I smell something else . . . like Bossy's stall before I clean it," she said. Everybody was trying to find a place to stand to see the circus. Virgie and Lottie slid through the crowd with Eddie and reached the front so Eddie could see.

Clowns tumbled into the ring as the ringmaster started the show. Eddie laughed and clapped his hands at their antics. Virgie turned to Lottie and said, "The clowns are funny, but it's more fun watching Eddie."

"The man doing somersaults on horseback is amazing," said Lottie. Then the trapeze artist entered the ring. "He is awfully brave to be so high off the ground," she said to Virgie, who nodded, and they both clapped enthusiastically for his act.

Virgie didn't care for the juggling. "Mr. Latch," she whispered, "I'm going to the outhouse. I'll be right back."

Mr. Latch nodded.

She left the tent, and as she turned the corner, she almost bumped into Danny and Joey Thompson. There was nothing to do but say, "Hi, Danny. Hi, Joey."

"Aw gee, Spider," Danny said. "Go away and don't talk to us. You'll just draw attention."

"We're going to slide under the tent flap. Now, go. Goodbye."

"How are you going to do that?" Virgie asked.

"Hey, you!" shouted a voice. "What are you doing? Stop trying to sneak in. We've had more than enough of that going on lately." A big man dressed in baggy brown pants with a dirty plaid shirt hanging out over his very large stomach came over to them. "You come with me."

"Wait," Virgie said. "I wasn't trying to sneak in. I—"

"Keep your story for the boss," interrupted the man. "From what I can see, you were with these two rascals. We'll see what Mr. Miles has to say about this."

The man grabbed Danny and Joey by their shoulders. "You follow," he said to Virgie. He led them to a circus wagon and knocked on the door. "Mr. Miles. I've got three for you. Caught them trying to sneak in."

The door opened. A long, thin face framed by a bushy black beard and wild curly hair peered around the door.

"Three thieves, you say," said Mr. Miles. He stepped down out of the wagon and stretched himself up to his six-foot, six-inch height. He was dressed all in black. He peered down at them.

"Now, what shall we do about this?" he asked the children.

Virgie could feel her knees knocking together, and she was afraid she was going to throw up on Mr. Miles' shiny black shoes. Finally, she found her voice. "I was not trying to sneak in," she said, looking way up at Mr. Miles. "I bought a ticket, and you can talk to Mr. Latch inside the tent and he'll show it to you."

Mr. Miles looked down at her and said to the man in the baggy pants, "Could this be true? Go find this Mr. Latch." Virgie told him where she had been standing.

"Now, what about you boys?" continued Mr. Miles.

Danny shoved his hands deep into his pants pockets and said with as much authority as his 12-year-old voice could muster, "We were not caught sneaking into the tent. We were standing outside visiting with Virgie. We go to school together."

"Is that true? Are you classmates?" Mr. Miles asked. Virgie and Joey both nodded their heads.

The man with the baggy pants returned with Mr. Latch, Lottie and Eddie in tow.

Virgie was relieved to see Mr. Latch with the tickets in his hand.

Mr. Miles looked at the tickets and then at Danny and Joey. "Where are *your* tickets?"

"We threw them on the ground after we entered the tent," Danny said firmly. "We didn't think we would need them again."

Mr. Miles looked at Lottie. "Do you know these two rascals?" he asked, pointing to Danny and Joey.

Lottie nodded. "We go to the same school."

"All right," Mr. Miles said. "You're off this time. But next time you two boys are caught outside my circus tent, I won't believe your story." He turned and climbed back into his wagon. The boys ran off.

Virgie looked up at Mr. Latch. "I'm sorry he had to find you," she said.

"I'm just glad I hadn't thrown the ticket stubs on the floor. Let's go watch the rest of the show," said Mr. Latch.

Soon Virgie was back in the tent and swallowed up by the crowd. By the end of the third clown act, she was laughing and clapping with the rest of them.

At the end of the night, when Mr. Latch dropped her off at her home, Virgie turned and called, "Thank you, again!" as she ran inside to report on her outing. "It was so much fun," she said. "The clowns were so funny, and the trapeze artist was very brave. I am glad I earned the money and went to it." She then reported on her run-in with Danny, Joey, and Monty Miles.

"You have to watch the friends you keep," said Papa.

Monday, August 9

Virgie stood outside the front door waiting for Lottie to arrive to walk to school. She saw Danny and Joey Thompson in the distance and was glad the boys would be walking ahead of them.

She looked across the field but still did not see her friend coming. It was unlike Lottie to be late. Finally, Virgie had to leave. She was walking down the dirt path when she heard Lottie calling her name. Virgie turned around and saw her friend running toward her. As she got closer, Virgie could see there was no smile on Lottie's face.

"Don't worry. We'll make it on time," Virgie said, seeking to reassure her friend.

"Oh, it's not that!" Lottie said, bursting into tears.

Virgie stopped and put her arm around her friend's shoulder. "What is it? What's happened?"

"My mother and brothers left on the stage yesterday morning for Faribault, where we used to live," Lottie blurted out through her tears. "I'm staying here to finish out the school term and help Pa with the housework. Mother was crying almost all day Saturday. And she and Pa would go into the bedroom and close the door. I could hear them talking, but I couldn't hear what they were saying. My father was really quiet yesterday, and he told me to go study when I tried to talk to him. I don't know what's happening," said Lottie through another heaving sob.

Virgie stared at her best friend. She did not know what to say. She didn't know what was happening or what it all meant. Lottie had said that her mother was often sad. And Virgie had not seen Lottie's mother around the village very much since the Fourth of July, when they had gone to the river for a picnic. Virgie remembered her mother saying Mrs. Latch wasn't feeling strong that day.

"What if my mother doesn't come back? That would be horrible," Lottie choked out. "I miss her so much."

Virgie could not imagine her world without her mother. Then she had what she knew was a most selfish thought: *What if Lottie and her father moved back to Faribault to be with her mother?* Virgie was sick at the thought of losing her best friend. Her only friend. The pain of leaving the Carnahan twins in Sioux Falls was still fresh in her mind.

But now Virgie knew she had to help Lottie stop crying because they saw other children ahead of them on the way to school. It would never do to have them asking questions. When they reached the school's well, Virgie pulled up fresh water in the pail and had Lottie splash it on her face. Then Virgie pulled a clean handkerchief from her apron pocket and helped Lottie wipe her face. When the two girls walked into the schoolhouse, only Lottie's red eyes would have given her away. Virgie was relieved that the students didn't notice Lottie's averted gaze.

After school, Virgie found her mother in the kitchen. "Do you know when Mrs. Latch will be coming back to Egan?" she asked.

"Well," replied Mama, "Papa told me over lunch that Mrs. Latch had gone for a long visit to Faribault." Newcomers to the prairie would sometimes return to their former homes because they missed their family, found the work too physically difficult, or thought the weather too harsh. The rest of the family soon followed.

"Lottie really misses her mother." Virgie was glad that she could talk to her mother about it.

"I'm sure," Mama said. "But Lottie is lucky to be able to finish out the school term here. When school is finished, she'll be busy with the cleaning and cooking. The time will go quickly until her mother returns." Virgie soon found her concern about Lottie overshadowed by events in the village.

Early Saturday morning the girls were pulling weeds in the garden. Other than the soft sound of roots being tugged from the earth, all was quiet. Suddenly, Ruth asked, "Do you hear something?" The girls stopped working and held their breath. They heard a low rumble in the distance and felt the ground tremble slightly.

Ruth stood up and cried, "Look at that brown cloud!" Virgie quickly stood and looked toward the east. Dust billowed skyward into a mass blocking the horizon. Thousands of head of cattle were moving the cloud slowly west along Roscoe Road.

They called their parents, and all watched as the cloud of dust drew closer. A lead rider kept the cattle from running too fast. Virgie could hear other riders softly calling to the cattle, "Move along, big fella" and "Step lively" as the never-ending stream of animals came down the road. And over the grunting and mooing, she could hear the clicking together of the horns of the large longhorns as their heads nodded and moved. There was a very gentle tremor in the ground as the heavy steers walked by.

"Quick, into the house so you don't breathe that dust!" Mama said, turning to go into the house. Everyone ran in. The windows helped keep some of the dust out of the house. But no one wanted to miss the parade of cattle coming down the road. Mama dipped dishtowels into a basin of water, wrung them out, and handed one to each as they went back outside. "Hold it over your nose to keep out the dust," she instructed. "Ben, stay in the house so that dust doesn't blow into your eyes."

But Papa had to go back out. "This is just too unbelievable," he said. They watched the cloud grow larger and pass within a block of their home. Papa's eyes did start watering again, and he had to spend the next day in the house with cold cloths over them. Then he was back at work.

Virgie felt as if her world were in constant motion that summer, as thousands of head of cattle and sheep, along with horses, oxen, wagons, carts, carriages, stagecoaches, houses, hotels, stores, and people all passed near her home along Roscoe Road. Wagons filled with lumber rumbled back and forth on Third Street, and the sound of hammers filled the air as men built more stores and businesses and houses. She thought of what Mr. Nelson had said that day when one hundred wagons passed the schoolhouse: "You are watching history in the making . . . the westward expansion of this country." *This must be what he meant*, Virgie thought.

Friday, August 20

Farmers needed their sons to harvest the wheat and oats, so the school term ended August 20. The harvesting season was especially good news for Papa. He had been coming home late every night for the past two weeks as he continued visiting farmers in a fifteen-mile radius and signing contracts for their wheat and oats. He was the happiest Virgie had ever seen him.

On the last day of school, the young scholars were performing a program for their families. That morning, Virgie asked Ruth to cut her bangs so her hair would look nice for the program. Ruth took the scissors, pressed Virgie's hair against her forehead, and carefully cut straight across, catching the long hair as it fell. Virgie took the towel and rubbed at her face to remove the itchy hair. Finally, she looked up at Ruth. "How do they look?"

"Very nice," Ruth replied. "That was a good idea. I might have Mary cut bangs for me also."

Parents of all twenty-three of the school's students came that afternoon for the exhibition. Virgie saw her parents and Mr. Latch among the many lined up along the classroom walls. The program included recitations, a spelling bee, and musical selections. Virgie felt her face turn red when, in an early round of the spelling bee, she misspelled the word "cemetery" as "cemetary." As she went to her seat, she murmured, "Cemetery with three e's, cemetery with three e's. I don't think I will ever forget that."

Lottie read "The Village Blacksmith" by Henry Wadsworth Longfellow:
"And children coming home from school
Look in at the open door;
They love to see the flaming forge,
And hear the bellows roar."

Lottie and Virgie smiled at each other. When Lottie was practicing the poem, she had said to Virgie, "I've never seen a spreading chestnut tree like the one in the poem, but I like walking by Mr. Jenson's blacksmith shop and watching him hammer on the hot horseshoes." Both girls loved the poem. Virgie felt sad for Lottie because Mrs. Latch wasn't there.

Mr. Nelson had asked Virgie to give her report on birds. Virgie unfolded the paper on which she had written, "Some birds are very pretty. I do not know very much about birds, but I am going to tell you all I know. The birds I know of are the robin, martin, blackbird, snowbird, hummingbird, kingbird, parrot, and eagle. The robins come very early in the spring. I think they are very pretty, and I like to have them come. Snowbirds are gray and white and hop about the doorstep picking up the crumbs and seeds. They seem happiest in a snowstorm. They stay with us all winter. I don't know where they go in the summertime."

Virgie took a breath and concluded her report with the eagle. "The eagle is the largest bird of all. They build their nests on high places. They feed on fish and meat." Then she sat down.

Lottie leaned across and whispered to Virgie, "Your report was interesting. And I like your bangs."

Virgie thought Ruth was the star of the class when she sang her song. Everyone applauded when she finished, and Virgie heard several comment that Ruth's voice was bell-like in its clarity.

Mr. Nelson thanked all for coming and reminded them of the meeting that night to vote on moving the schoolhouse to Egan.

As the Vandenbergs left school, they looked at the schoolhouse. The stores had all been moved to Egan. "Do you think they'll move the schoolhouse?" Virgie asked Mama.

"They should," Mama said. "The children are in Egan."

They saw the DeBoers on the way home. "See you tomorrow," Mr. DeBoer called to Papa.

"What's tomorrow?" asked Virgie.

"I'm hunting prairie chickens with him and Mr. Barnard," Papa replied. "I'll walk the fields and help flush the birds, but I'm not going to take my shotgun. My eyes are watering badly again. I don't think I see well enough to shoot a gun. But I'll have a share of the birds."

Papa had already left Saturday morning when Virgie and Ruth walked to Mr. Mann's office to find out the election results. "They're moving the schoolhouse. It was unanimous," Mr. Mann said. "A committee will find a site and arrange for the move. It should be this fall, girls."

"That's wonderful news, Mr. Mann," said Virgie.

"I'm sure we'll not miss the two-mile walk in the middle of winter," added Ruth.

Saturday night, Papa walked through the door with three prairie chickens. "We had a good hunt," he said as he took off his jacket. "Those prairie chickens are funny birds. When flushed, they fly a short distance and then they land and sit. They don't run like pheasants. They make for an easy prey."

He spent the evening plucking the feathers and cleaning the birds. Virgie and Ruth helped Mama break up bread into small pieces for the dressing. Their mother seasoned it with sage, salt, and pepper. They left the pan of bread pieces on the table to dry overnight. The next morning, Mama cooked some chopped onion in butter and stirred the mixture into the breadcrumbs. Then she cut up the prairie chickens, put the pieces in a roaster, and spooned in the dressing. "Oh," sighed Virgie as the birds roasted, "that dressing smells wonderful. Isn't it time to eat?"

Monday, August 23
It rained all day, so Mama and the girls worked in the

cellar organizing the food jars on the shelves Papa had built against the earthen walls. Glass jars of dried green peas stood lined up next to the jewel-red jars of raspberry jam they'd made from fruit picked in late July along a river ravine. Virgie swept the dirt floor clean to ready it for the provisions they would store this week.

The next morning Mama handed the girls two baskets. "Take these down to the riverbank and gather all the ripe plums you can find." The girls ran off and filled their baskets.

Virgie alternately dragged and carried her basket home because it was so heavy. Her arms stung from the scratches of the plum branches.

Mama came out and looked at the full baskets. She would cook the plums into plum jelly, plum syrup sweetener, and plum-apple butter.

That evening, Papa walked into the house with a shout. "Look what I got today," he said. "Fresh corn on the cob for dinner!" Many parts of the corn plant were useful to the settlers. Shaved corn kernels would be dried, and the parched corn would be stored in paper sacks and hung from bedroom rafters to be used for corn soup in the winter. The tops of dried stalks could be used for bedding, and the stalks would insulate the upstairs bedrooms. The cobs would be dried and stored to use as fuel if needed, or the settlers would use them in the outhouses as paper.

Mama and the girls were threading green beans on the side porch the next day when Papa surprised them and came home for lunch. "This was not a good day," he said. "I needed cash to buy supplies, so I took eggs, some chickens, and several blocks of Mama's butter to sell. The man paid for them with this five-dollar gold piece that I have since discovered is a fake. It is dated 1880 and feels and looks exactly like a five-dollar gold piece, but it is not." He explained that the edges were genuine gold, so it would stand the acid test, but it had no ring. That meant the filling wasn't gold. The coin had been slit into, hollowed out, and filled with a cheap material. Only the shell was genuine gold. "It's the latest swindle, and I was tricked out of five big ones. Mr. Mann is going to warn his readers."

That afternoon, Mama and the girls finished threading the beans on a strong string. These would be hung, along with the sacks of parched corn, from the rafters of the bedrooms and allowed to dry. This would be the family's first winter out on the prairie, with few buildings and trees to shelter them from the wind and snow. As they worked, Mama shared with the girls her concerns about preserving and storing adequate food for the long winter months. How many stores would carry groceries? How often would the train bring supplies to the small village?

When the Vandenbergs left church services in the hardware store that hot and humid Sunday afternoon, they saw a dark purple bank of clouds stretched across the horizon in the west. They hurried home. Virgie watched as the cloudbank methodically erased the blue from the sky.

At the first rumble of thunder, she called to Papa, "Shouldn't we go to the cellar?"

"Not a bad idea, Virgie," Papa replied. He grabbed a kerosene lantern. Before closing the door, Papa lit the lantern so they could see the shelves of canned fruits and vegetables. "We don't want to break any of those glass jars and lose our winter food supply," he said.

Virgie headed for her haven under the stairs and against the wall. She closed her eyes and squeezed her hands into tight fists, frightened that another tornado would roar into Egan. But this storm hit Egan with a thunderous crash and no tornado. Lightning cracked, and wind tore at the cellar door. When it was over, the family emerged from the cellar into a soft rain.

"Look, Virgie," Papa said. "Everything is fine. I don't see any damage." Egan had escaped.

When Papa came home for lunch on Monday, he said, "I didn't realize how lucky we were with that storm yesterday. Remember the railroad workers finishing the road here? Those same men are laying track about two miles south of here. Last night they were preparing to go to bed in the train cars when the storm hit. It tore the cars from the rope moorings and threw them into a ditch. One car was completely destroyed and the other two were badly wrecked."

"Were the men hurt?" Ruth asked.

"One man had his leg crushed and his collar bone broken. Another dislocated his shoulder and was badly bruised. Others weren't as seriously hurt. They're lucky no one was killed," Papa said. "We don't need any more rain."

That afternoon, the girls walked to the river and filled their baskets with wild grapes. Virgie also found a patch of milkweed with the green pods just turning brown. She picked about two dozen pods and put them on top of the grapes. She had a special use for them at Christmas. On the way home, they met Lottie.

"Can you play?" she asked.

Virgie shook her head. "I wish I could. Mama has us working from sunup to sundown getting ready for winter. Aren't you and your Pa busy stocking up?"

Lottie shook her head. "He says there's no need to worry."

The girls spent Tuesday morning digging carrots and onions. As Virgie and Ruth cleaned up after lunch, they were surprised to hear horses pulling a cart into the yard. Papa usually walked to work or rode out to the claims on Dusty. As they ran out the door, they heard him call, "Give me a hand with these." Virgie stared at the piles of potatoes, turnips, parsnips, and cabbages in the cart. Papa explained, "Farmers are bringing their vegetables to town to sell. I bought these."

Mama came out the door with baskets in hand. "Those look good," she said. "Spread the potatoes on the grass to dry. Don't clean them. They will keep better with bits of soil still clinging to them. Then, girls, fill these baskets with the other vegetables and carry them to the cellar."

Ruth dug up the dirt in the cellar floor and buried the turnips. Virgie stuck the cabbages in the corner dirt pile with their roots sticking out. Papa rolled down a barrel and filled it with sand to store the parsnips.

Virgie was tired, hot, and dirty by the time she finished burying the cabbages. After supper, she splashed water on her face and arms and crawled into bed.

She and Ruth rose early Wednesday morning to finish digging the onions and carrots, which need to dry during the heat of the day.

"I really don't see why we have to do all this. We didn't have to work this hard in Sioux Falls. Lottie and her Pa aren't worried at all," Virgie said to Ruth as they scattered the carrots.

"You're right, Virgie," Mama said as she walked out onto the porch. "But most people in the village are working hard. We have to. We don't know what kind of supplies the stores will have."

Mama looked at their morning's work. "It's going to be hot this afternoon. You've done a good job. Why don't you take a break until it's time to help with supper."

Virgie washed up and said she was going to go to Lottie's. She went upstairs and took off her faded gingham work dress. It was smeared with dirt, with bits of dried soil and wilted leaves clinging to it from two days of storing root vegetables and digging onions and carrots. She pulled on her other work dress, picked up her hairbrush, and sat down on the bed to work on the tangles. When Virgie awoke two hours later, she couldn't remember lying down.

1880

September

A Secret Project

Thursday, September 2

That night, Papa brought home not vegetables but a barrel of apples that had just arrived at Barnard's. "Oh, good," Virgie said. "Apples are my favorite."

When Virgie came into the kitchen early the next morning, Ruth was already carrying baskets of unblemished apples to the cellar.

Virgie's assignment was cutting blemishes out of the remaining apples. She loved the crisp sound as the knife sliced through the apple and released the sweet aroma that soon enveloped the warm kitchen. Mama mixed apple pieces with plums for her special plum butter. She also cooked chunks for apple butter, which she poured into stoneware jars.

They peeled, cored, and sliced other apples before drying them in the sun. When they broke for lunch, Virgie asked Mama, "Could I take some of these cores and feed them to Dusty and Pal?" Mama nodded, and Virgie went out to the barn. She held the cores flat in her hand. She loved the softness of the horses' velvety lips as they ate from her hand. And their long whiskers tickled her wrists. "That's a treat you haven't had for a while, isn't it?" she said to the horses as she stroked their noses.

That afternoon, Virgie helped Mama prepare cores and peelings for making cider vinegar. They placed the apple pieces in a stone crock, covered them with water, and put a plate on top. They would be kept in a warm place for two weeks or more.

"We've done enough cooking for today," said Mama late that afternoon as they cleaned up. "Ruth, why don't you set out some cold meat and bread for supper?"

"Not for me," said Virgie, taking off her apron. "I'm too tired to eat, and I never want to see another apple. I ache all over." She curled up in her bed and slept for fourteen hours.

Friday morning, Mama said the remaining apples could wait a day. "We need a break. We'll just do a load of wash, and then we'll be done working for the day. I already have water heating outside over the fire. I put the clothes to soak when I got up. I think it's hot enough so you two can grate a bar of lye soap and wash our work dresses. They need a good cleaning."

Virgie walked outside with Ruth to the big cast-iron laundry pot. "What are you going to do today?" she asked Ruth, as they stirred the lye soap into the water.

"I'm going to meet Maggie O'Brien at Mary's house to plan a sociable," Ruth said. "We'll want to have singing and dancing so we need to think of a couple of musicians to invite."

"Who's Maggie O'Brien?" Virgie asked.

"She just moved here. Her mother opened Molly's Restaurant and Confectionery Store," Ruth replied. "Maggie helps her mother bake pies and cakes for the restaurant. Her father died just after the war."

When they added their clothes to the water, they

knocked the air bubbles out of them with a big stick and swished them around. They took the laundry stick and lifted out the dresses to find the stains. They put a solid bar of lye soap at the top of the washboard, rubbed the soiled clothing over the soap, and vigorously scrubbed the clothes on the ribbed surface of the washboard. When they were satisfied the clothes were clean, they carried them over to the stand that held the rinse tub and the wringer. They put the clothes into the cold water and then fed them through the wringer to squeeze out the water.

As they were wringing the clothes, Papa walked by. "I know what I need to do this week," he said. "I have to build a lean-to next to the house for the laundry tubs. You can't be outside in the winter washing clothes."

"That will be good," said Virgie as they started hanging the dresses on the clothesline.

When finished with the clothes, Virgie met Lottie, and they walked into town to ask Mr. Mann about the plans for moving the schoolhouse to Egan.

"It's not good news, girls," he said when they found him in his office at the newspaper. "The men are busy with the harvest and can't move the schoolhouse for at least a month."

As they were leaving, Virgie spied old clothes piled in the corner of the office. "What are those?" she asked Mr. Mann.

"Oh," he said, "those were dropped off by one of the families heading west. They were getting rid of things. The clothes are clean but worn. I haven't decided yet what to do with them."

Virgie had an idea. "Could we have them, Mr. Mann? I promise we'll put them to good use."

"Well, I suppose," he said. "Just don't waste them."

As they left the office with clothes spilling out of their arms, Lottie said, "What are you thinking of, Virgie? What are we going to do with these?"

"Let's carry them home, and then I'll tell you," Virgie replied.

They lugged the clothes into Virgie's room and dumped them on her bed.

"Now," Virgie said. "I'll tell you what we'll do. Mama said she would not teach me lace making until I learned to sew better stitches. And you said you feel drafts around your door on windy mornings. We can sew together squares of cloth like a quilt and make doormats. It will be our secret project."

Virgie helped Lottie take a pile of the clothes to her house and carry them into Lottie's bedroom. When Lottie's mother left for Minnesota, she took the extra bedding that had been stored in Lottie's bedroom. "There's room in this chest for the clothes, and Pa won't ever see them," she said.

The two girls sat on Lottie's bed and discussed their project and what else they would need, such as padding and backing. "I'll see what I can find here to use," said Lottie.

So Virgie and Lottie started their secret project.

Later that week, Virgie noticed differences in the air from the heat and humidity of early September. On some mornings she could feel a hint of crispness in the breezes out of the north.

"Things are changing," Mama said as they stood in the yard hanging clothes on the line. "Look at the sky, Virgie. The white puffy clouds of summer are gone. The clouds have flattened out like gray sheets. It's another sign of the coming season."

Two mornings later, Virgie awoke to the sound of footsteps crunching outside her window.

Wednesday, September 8

Virgie hopped out of bed and ran to the window. She saw Papa walking off to work. With each step he created a dark trail of footprints on the white grass. Heavy coats of frost pulled the tall prairie grasses to the ground, and the early sun turned them a golden pink. White feathery crystals of ice, glistening in the sun's rays, stretched along the clotheslines in the yard. In the distance, the trees in the grove shimmered in their white beauty, and the black ribbon of the river wrapped it all up. "It's beautiful," Virgie murmured. "And it's cold!" She suddenly realized she had nothing on her feet and the bare floors felt like ice. She danced across the floor, jumped back into her warm bed, and pulled up the covers.

Then she remembered why Papa was heading off so early. His warehouse was opening today.

She got up, took off the top of the packing barrel, and pulled out a woolen dress and slipped it on. *Oh, this feels so nice. It's still warm from the summer heat,* she thought to herself. She pulled on wool stockings and buttoned her shoes. Then she went downstairs to find Mama writing at the kitchen table.

"What are you doing?" asked Virgie.

"I'm writing a note to Aunt Maud in Albert Lea and inviting her and the children here for a few days in October. They could come by train. Papa said last night that the telegraph wires were stretched to Egan yesterday. The telegraph office should be open today."

"Oh, did you hear that?" Virgie said to Ruth as she walked into the kitchen. "Eddie and Nell are coming to visit in October."

"Wait a minute," said Mama, laughing. "I'm inviting them. We have to wait for their answer."

Later that week, Papa said he would be gone from the house on Saturday. "A group of us decided to build a bridge over the river east of town," he said. He explained that when there is a heavy rain, like there was early last week, the farmers weren't able to cross the river with their teams and wagons. With the snow melt next spring, it would be impossible for teams to cross. "We don't want business going to Flandreau because the farmers can't reach us."

That Saturday, Virgie, Ruth, and Mary walked down to the river to watch. It was a gray, cloudy day. Over the hammering, Virgie heard a sound. "Listen. What's that noise?" she asked. The girls looked around and saw nothing unusual. Then they noticed that the men had stopped working and were looking up at the sky. The girls followed their gaze and saw a flock of Canadian geese flying in a V shape and honking noisily.

The geese had barely passed over them when the girls heard shouts of "Look!" and "No, look over there!" Flocks of geese on their right, on their left, and directly overhead all flying south. Their honking created a terrible racket. No one moved. Heads tilted backward, they all watched openmouthed. Almost immediately after one wave of geese disappeared south into the horizon, more waves came out of the north, and as they came closer, the flocks took on the defined V formation. When the last flock disappeared into the sky to the south, heads dropped and the girls could hear excited conversations going on among the men.

"That was beautiful," marveled Virgie. "I've never seen anything like it."

Papa was tired when he came home that night. "I don't think we'll finish the bridge before winter," he said. "It's taking longer than we thought, and we can't work full-time on it because we're so busy with our regular jobs."

"We told Mama about the geese," said Virgie.

"It was amazing," he said, stroking his mustache. "But folks are worried. It's a little early in the birds' migration season. I hope this doesn't mean an early winter."

The next week, another hard frost left a thick coating of ice on everything.

With the hard frost and most of the vegetables now stored, Virgie and Lottie had time to work on their secret project. Sometimes they would sew at Virgie's house. But more often, she would tuck her cloth pieces into a basket, cover them, and walk to Lottie's, where they could work while her father was at the store.

"This is miserable weather," Virgie said as she shook water off her coat Wednesday afternoon. "We've had an awful lot of rain. It's either a steady drizzle or it pours. And it's cold out," she said with a shiver. "I'm glad it's toasty warm in your kitchen."

They cut the clothes into squares, sewed them together, and talked. Lottie said, "Mother is writing to me, but Pa still won't answer any questions. I don't know what's going to happen."

"Why don't you tell him how miserable you are?" Virgie asked.

"I don't want to worry him," said Lottie. "He's so busy with the store. So I keep still."

Virgie wanted to make Lottie laugh and smile again. She talked about games such as charades and activities such as ice skating they might do that winter. As the days passed, the first doormats took shape. "We can cut rectangles out of these old blankets to use as padding," Lottie said. She found a stack of flour sacks in the kitchen that she knew her father didn't need. The girls used the sacks as backing for the doormats.

Monday, September 27

That afternoon, Virgie said, "Let's take a break and walk down Third Street to see what's new." They stopped and watched wagons loaded with new supplies going back and forth between the train tracks and the stores. The street was one hundred feet wide, so wagons and carts could easily be turned around in the street.

"Hi, Danny. Hi, Joey," Virgie called. The brothers were unloading a wagon in front of Barnard's.

"Oh, no," groaned Danny. "Not Spider again."

"Oh, stop calling me names. This conversation is getting old," Virgie retorted as they walked by.

The girls walked up to Barnard's door. They stopped. "Wait a minute," Virgie said. "We don't want to go in there. Look how crowded it is."

"That's right," said Mr. Mann, who was right behind them. "After the farmers sell their crops to your father, they come here to shop. This is an exciting time. Come back next week. It won't be so crowded. Two more general stores are opening. Even more exciting, Thursday's paper will have the story that C.C. Johnson, hotel proprietor from back east, plans to build a first-class hotel here."

Later that week, Virgie and Lottie decided to go with Mama to one of the new stores, Epton Kennedy's General Store, which specialized in groceries and would accept fresh local produce and foods in trade. Virgie wrapped blocks of freshly churned butter while Mama gently placed eggs in another basket.

"I hope Mr. Kennedy will want to buy butter," Mama said as they walked with their baskets to the store. "I read in *The Egan Express* that there is something new called oleomargarine that will take the place of butter. I don't see how it can be as good."

They had just reached Third Street when they heard shouting.

Mama, Virgie, and Lottie looked down the street in time to see a team of horses with a carriage charging down the street. The driver ran behind, waving his arms and yelling at his horses to stop. "Back up!" Mama shouted. The three backed up flat against the building as the runaway team flew by them, heading east toward the river, its driver racing after them.

The thunder of the charging hooves, the racket of the carriage wheels, the cries of the driver, and the screams of bystanders created all the alarm needed for those still along the street. Mama, Virgie, and Lottie watched the scene unfold as people jumped to the left and to the right to escape the horses.

"That was close," Mama said. They caught their breath and went into Latch's Hardware Store, where the Egan Post Office was now located. Lottie greeted her father.

"Hello, Virgie, Mrs. Vandenberg," said Mr. Latch. Mama asked if she had a letter. "You have one from Minnesota," he said, handing it to her.

"It's good news," said Mama, reading. "Aunt Maud and her children are coming in mid-October, after the harvest and while the weather is still good."

Next, the three walked to Epton Kennedy's General Store.

Virgie was the first to spot the barrel of fresh cranberries. "Look," she called to Mama. "We can make cranberry sauce."

Mama agreed and bought a peck of cranberries. The berries would store well in the cellar if they were kept in a covered container with water.

Virgie picked up a jug of syrup. Mr. Kennedy said, "Mr. Nelson makes that syrup from his sugar cane. It's almost like molasses. Mighty tasty."

"Mr. Nelson's my teacher," Virgie said. "Can we please try some, Mama?"

She agreed, adding the syrup to her order for Papa to pick up later.

Mr. Kennedy was pleased to trade for the fresh butter and eggs. "That was a good deal," said Mama as they walked out of the store. "He credited me 25 cents a pound for the butter."

1880
October

Stranded in the Snow

Friday, October 1

As they sat around the table after supper, Papa fingered his mustache. His face turned grim. "Those hard rains we had last month came before much of the prairie grass had been cut and stacked. The farmers are saying they don't think there will be enough hay to supply the demand."

"What does that mean?" asked Virgie, feeling very uneasy. She knew Papa was very serious when he started playing with the curl at the end of his mustache.

"It could mean we would run out of hay for our animals to eat before spring comes," replied Papa. "I'm going to see if there is a farmer who will sell some hay. If I can find it, you girls will have to help stack it this weekend. I'll also want to buy enough oats for the animals and corn for the chickens to see us through the winter."

When the girls got up Saturday morning, Papa was already gone. About midmorning, he pulled into the yard. The cart was filled with loose hay. Virgie and Ruth ran out. "Here," he said. "After I dump this, stack it around the post by the barn. I'm going out to buy another load." Mama grabbed a pitchfork from the porch and came to help. On his fourth and last trip, Papa brought oats and corn, which they shoveled into barrels inside the barn. At the end of the day, Virgie was exhausted, but felt proud of what she had done to help the animals.

The following Wednesday, it was almost 9:30 in the evening when he walked in. The girls ran into the kitchen to hear why he was so late. "It was an unbelievable day," he said, sinking onto a kitchen chair. "The warehouse took in more than one thousand bushels of wheat. I didn't have a moment's rest. And I wasn't the only busy one. I heard that Bradly Brothers Lumber sold nineteen thousand feet of lumber. They couldn't load any more!"

After he ate some dinner, he sat at the table talking to Mama. Virgie was washing up his dishes and saw a worried look cross his face. Again, his hand played with his mustache. She heard him say, "We're going to have problems if we can't buy coal and wood for fuel for the winter. There was no coal on the latest train. Hasn't been any for a week now. I don't understand why. I'm going to search the grove in my spare time and pick up dead logs and branches I find. We might have to find our own fuel.

I'm glad we're drying the cow dung. We can burn that if we need to. You girls need to gather up dried cow pies from the cattle drives and bring them to the barn."

Virgie wiped her hands and thought of what she had just heard. She had never been through a winter with no fuel. She could not imagine her home being really cold. How would they cook their food? She knew Papa was very serious.

At the start of the next week, Mama began preparing for Aunt Maud's visit. They needed to clean the house, air the bedding, and start the baking. As they worked, they talked about all they could show their cousins.

"Could we go to the horse race Saturday? I heard they raised thirty dollars for the winning horses, so there'll be a big crowd," said Ruth. Mama agreed it sounded like fun.

By the end of the week, they were ready. The train was to arrive at 11:35 Friday night.

Friday, October 15

As Virgie rolled out the sugar cookie dough Friday morning, she looked out the kitchen window. She thought she saw a snowflake. She looked harder and saw nothing. She went back to her cookie dough. When she looked up again, she knew it was not her imagination. The air was filled with swirling snowflakes. She felt the excitement drain out of her. She was worried about her cousins, who were on the train heading into the storm.

A stiff, cold wind accompanied the snow that blew into drifts around the house. Virgie poked her head out the front door to see if she wanted to go outside and play. She quickly drew it back in as the north wind blew sharp icy particles at her face.

Papa came home mid-afternoon. He stood by the cooking stove and warmed his hands. He said there was nothing to do at the warehouse. "Only the farmers who left early this morning reached Egan," he said. "I think some who lived nearby made it home safely. But several are spending the night with friends here."

Papa turned to go back out the door. "I didn't think I would need to put a rope between the house and the barn this early in the season," he said, "but this snow today makes me think I had better be prepared." In heavy blizzards, settlers could lose sight of buildings and wander out on the prairie and become lost. The girls watched him secure a rope between the two buildings.

When Virgie went to bed that night, she wondered if the train would make it in the next day.

In the morning, she had her answer before she got out of bed. She could hear it. Overnight, the stiff wind from Friday had turned into a howling gale that shrieked as it hit the northwest corner of their house. She got out of bed and looked out the window. The winds were whipping the snow into a freezing frenzy. She could not see the village through the whirling snow.

She dressed quickly and went downstairs into the warmth of the kitchen. She had just sat down at the table when Papa and a cloud of snow blew in the door. "It's tough out there," he said, handing the pail of well water to Mama and brushing off the snow from his clothes. "The air is so cold and full of snow, it's hard to be out in it for very long. I took care of Bossy and the horses and put the feed and water out for the chickens. I'm glad I put that rope up yesterday."

To Virgie's unasked question, Mama shook her head. "No, I don't think they'll arrive today," she said. Virgie got her basket of fabric pieces, sat by the stove, and sewed on the squares for the doormat, telling Mama she was practicing her stitches. Virgie was stitching her second doormat.

The blizzard raged until Sunday morning. Papa headed out to the barn to take care of the animals. "We've had about two feet of snow, I'd guess. I added a rope from the side porch to the outhouse and to the well so we can safely walk out there," he said on his return.

Virgie looked out across the prairie. It was white for mile upon endless mile, and the ground became one with the gray clouds on the horizon.

Papa walked to the depot to check on the status of the train. "It's not good news," he said when he returned. "The train passed the stationmaster in Fulda, Minnesota, but didn't show up in Chandler. They think it's stuck somewhere west of Fulda. Crews are out looking for it.

"The old settlers at Mrs. Cummings' Rooming House are saying they've never seen a storm this bad so early in the season," Papa continued. "It really caught people unprepared."

Virgie thought how scared her cousins must be and wondered if their train had been found. On Monday, Papa reported that crews had delivered food to the train passengers and were clearing the tracks. "But it'll still be a couple of days before the train arrives," he said.

They were all worried about their cousins. But they were somewhat cheered when the sun came out and warming temperatures started to melt the snow.

On Wednesday morning, Papa ran home. "The train's on its way," he announced.

The Vandenbergs stood in the warmth of the sun by the railroad boarding car, which was serving as the temporary depot. They finally saw the train, snow still packed up against the engine, as it chugged into the village. Then they saw Aunt Maud, Eddie, and Nell at the windows waving.

Virgie smiled and waved as she watched them descend the steps of the train. She had not seen Eddie and Nell since her family had visited Albert Lea five years ago. The cousins all stood looking at each other. Nell was no longer twelve years old, but a young woman of seventeen, with thick chestnut-colored hair pulled back in a bun. Little Eddie had lost his cherubic looks. He was a lanky twelve-year-old with the cowlicks in his brown hair not quite tamed.

"Welcome to Egan!" said Mama, breaking the silence and hugging the three of them. "You must be exhausted and hungry," Mama said. "We want to hear all about your trip, but wait until we reach the house and you can warm up and have something to eat." Papa helped pile the valises into the cart, leaving just enough room for the travelers, Mama, and himself. Ruth and Virgie ran the few blocks to their home.

The kitchen was warm and toasty from the heat of the stove, where a large pot of split pea and ham bone soup simmered on the back burner. Mama served steaming bowls of soup with large slabs of fresh bread. Everyone gathered around to hear the travelers' tales.

"I'm so glad to be here," Aunt Maud said. "We left Albert Lea on time, and at first the train ride was quite smooth. Then it started snowing, and the train went slower and slower. We got stuck several times, but the crew always got us going again. The stationmaster in Fulda said he thought we could make it to the next town, where there were better accommodations. But we couldn't.

"Friday evening the train couldn't go any farther. We had no idea where we were. We couldn't see anything but white flakes pounding the windows. It was like being in a giant white cocoon. I told Eddie and Nell to eat lightly for dinner because the train might become stuck. So we had the leftovers for Saturday breakfast, and they tasted awfully good."

Aunt Maud said the basket of gifts she had brought to the family was empty. Her loaves of apple bread, pound cakes, jars of strawberry jam, and jars of pickles became part of the community larder along with contributions of bread, dried beef strips, and apples from others.

"The passengers took inventory of what we all had and divided it into portions for Saturday and Sunday with a little left in case we needed it Monday. We were never full, but our stomachs didn't growl."

"Weren't you cold?" asked Ruth.

"Not very," Aunt Maud said. "We all sat close to the stove at the end of the train car, which gave off some heat. The trainmen brought out buffalo robes for us, and they kept us warm."

"When did they find the train?" asked Ruth.

"The train crews made it through to us Sunday night and brought baskets of meat sandwiches," Eddie answered. "Then we knew we would be safe."

"Wasn't it boring sitting in the train all that time?" asked Virgie.

"It was at first," Eddie answered. "But once the storm stopped, there was lots of activity. I helped shovel snow away from the train. There were drifts ten feet high, so I had to be careful not to go too far off the track."

"That is scary," said Virgie with a shudder.

Nell continued: "Most amazingly, there was a sod house buried under the snow in a ravine near the tracks. On Sunday morning, I was looking out the window and saw a man come out of this huge snowbank. He had cut a hole in his roof in order to climb out of the house. Then we watched as he and his wife dug a tunnel toward his stable, which was also buried. The train crew told us he reached his animals just before dark."

On Thursday, the sun turned the snow such a brilliant white that it hurt Virgie's eyes to look in the distance. But the sun provided some warmth, and the snow continued to melt except in sheltered areas. Lottie came over and met the cousins. The three girls took Eddie and Nell on a tour of the town, past all 23 businesses and 20 homes and the town well.

The melting snow had turned dirt into mud on Third Street. Several heavily loaded wagons were sunk up to the hubs of their wheels in mud. The young people kept their eyes on the ground as they stepped gingerly along the street, the girls lifting their long skirts, searching for snow surfaces or spots of gravel put down by the merchants. Virgie looked up for a second and gave a shout of glee. "Look! A sidewalk!" A new wooden sidewalk had been constructed in front of Barnard's. "Isn't this wonderful?" she exclaimed as they clattered along on the boards.

Back at the house, the four girls took over the parlor to visit and play charades, one of Virgie's favorites. Later, they settled down by the stove and just talked. Ruth wanted to hear all about Nell's plans to be a teacher.

"Where will you teach?" Ruth asked.

"I'm not sure," Nell said. "School districts near Albert Lea are always looking for teachers. I've also thought about coming to Dakota Territory. This trip was a rough introduction, but the openness of the land is beautiful."

"Teaching sounds interesting," Ruth said. "I might like to teach music somewhere. It will be interesting to see what Mr. Nelson does with music next term. But, enough of that. Tell us about our grandparents and other cousins," she said. "We've missed a lot these past five years."

"I miss Grandmama and Grandpapa," Virgie said. She thought of Grandmama bustling around the kitchen as the fragrance of baking bread filled the farmhouse. And she remembered how cozy she felt in the gentle warmth of the barn when she went with Grandpapa to feed the cows.

Grandmama and Grandpapa were doing well, Nell reported. "But Uncle Edmond and Aunt Mary and their six children are having a hard time. Sylvia and Effie were ill last winter," she said of their cousins. "And the sickness left them deaf. They can hear nothing."

"How awful," Ruth said. "How do they communicate with each other?"

"That's the hard part," Nell said. "They can talk to the rest of the family, but they can't hear the responses. You can imagine how difficult that is for all of them. The girls will have to leave home and go to the school for the deaf in Faribault."

Nell said the mental stress of having two deaf daughters, caring for a toddler son, managing a household of eight people, and preparing for winter was too much for Aunt Mary. "She couldn't handle it," said Nell. With two of the girls at Faribault, Uncle Edmond was going to see if relatives could take the other three girls, and they would put little Henry, who just turned two, up for adoption.

Virgie and Ruth sat in silence as they thought about what they had just heard. The quiet was broken by thumps coming from outside the house. The girls looked out the windows. Papa and Eddie were mounding dirt and prairie sod around the foundation of the house. "Papa said we had to bank the house to block out the wind and keep the food in the cellar from freezing," Ruth told Nellie. "It's nice of Eddie to help."

"It certainly is," Virgie said. "If not, we'd be out there shoveling dirt. Maybe he could live with us and help Papa with the chores."

The next day, the girls helped Eddie and Papa move the log pile close to the kitchen door. "Let's move the hay into the barn, too," Papa said. "It will be easier to feed the animals during a blizzard. That storm last week has caused me to rethink our preparations out here." They moved the dried cow pies from the sheltered side of the barn to an inside corner.

Virgie could not believe how quickly the days were passing. She heard Mama and Aunt Maud talk about the return trip to Albert Lea. Her cousins had to be home in time for the school term.

When the day arrived, Eddie and Nellie brought the valises to the kitchen. Mama handed Aunt Maud her basket. "Here," she said, "I've packed lots of food in your basket so you'll have plenty to eat if you get stuck again. I made our mother's oatmeal cookies." Aunt Maud smiled and nodded.

Virgie helped load the valises and baskets onto the carriage. Since the train going east left the station at 1:30 in the morning, Mama decided she and the girls would stay at home and Papa would drive the visitors to the depot.

As she hugged Aunt Maud goodbye, Virgie could smell the lily of the valley scent in her aunt's powder, and it reminded her of being rocked as a little girl in her aunt's lap. Virgie felt tears welling up as she thought of that warmth and love. She gave Aunt Maud an extra-tight hug.

Then she hugged Nell and Eddie. The girls sent the guests off in a flurry of waves. As the girls went up to bed, Virgie said quietly, "The house seems terribly empty now, doesn't it?"

Alone in her room, she carefully took down her toy teapot from the shelf. She removed the lid and pulled out the folded piece of paper and short pencil stub she stored there. She unfolded the paper and looked at her row of tally marks. She added another mark and counted them up: twenty-two marks, one for each week since their arrival. She was almost halfway through her year in Egan.

November

Life at Twenty Degrees Below Zero

Thursday, November 4

Snow had returned Wednesday, and a strong north wind had kept everyone inside. But this morning, when Virgie walked to the barn to feed the chickens and gather the eggs, she thought what a nice day it was. The air was cold and crisp, but the sun was out, the snow had stopped, and the wind had died down. *Funny,* she thought. *A month ago, I would not have thought this a nice day at all.*

When she returned to the house, Mama had another errand for her.

"Would you please go down to the post office and see if we have any mail? I haven't heard from the Albert Lea people since Aunt Maud's visit."

Virgie hurried off, but it wasn't long before she returned empty-handed, except for the latest edition of

The Egan Express. "It just came off the press. Mr. Mann handed it to me."

"No mail again?" Mama asked.

"No mail," Virgie said. "Not for us, not for anyone in town. Mr. Latch said the mail isn't being delivered to Egan. He said the stage driver told him the river is too high and the water too cold to put the horses through it. But Mr. Latch said there hasn't been a day in the past two weeks that other teams haven't crossed the river. He said if other teams can cross, so could the mail stage. He thinks that they just don't care about our mail service."

Mama sat at the table and opened the paper. "Oh, no," she said. "Two people died down near Elk Point in that last blizzard. Mr. Mann has the story in his paper. Here, I'll read it to you. 'A week ago Monday the bodies of Mrs. Lundquist and her four-year-old son were found in the snow two miles northwest of Big Springs in this county. Mrs. Lundquist was a widow living alone in the house with her son. As near as can be ascertained, during the fearful storm of Friday night, the house caught fire. She removed the boy from the house, a safe distance from the fire, wrapped him up in a robe, and returned to the house to save the furniture. She worked until she sank exhausted in the snow beside the house where her body was found three days later. The boy's body was found where she had laid him. Of all the accidents of the late storm, this is by far the saddest.'"

"Oh," Virgie said. "Those poor people."

Papa walked into the kitchen and said men in the town were going to work on the bridge again on Saturday. "If we work hard, we might be able to finish it. Teams could cross by next week," he said.

The next day, Ruth threw open the kitchen door and said breathlessly, "Mama, Mary is having a candy pull Saturday night. Can I please go?" At a candy pull, the party-goers butter their hands, gather up a ball of slightly cooled syrup and, using both hands, pull it as far as they can reach, fold it over, and repeat. This is done several times until the candy stiffens and ropes of candy can be pulled off.

"I don't see why not," Mama said. "Be careful of the hot syrup. Make sure you let it cool a bit before you start pulling it."

"Are Lottie and I invited?" asked Virgie.

"I'm sorry," Ruth said. "But she's just inviting people our age."

Virgie didn't think that was fair. She had never been to a candy pull, and it sounded like fun. Then she grinned and said, "Is Tom Gorseth invited?" Ruth gave a big smile in return. Virgie had seen Ruth and Tom talking at lunch and after school, and she had been teasing Ruth about having a crush on Tom.

Early Saturday morning, the winds whistled as they hit the frame house. The work on the bridge was canceled. But by early afternoon, the winds had died down, so Papa said he would take the horses and cart to search for more wood down by the river.

"Aren't the trains bringing coal?" asked Virgie.

"No," Papa said. He was worried about having enough fuel to last through the winter. But when he came back late that afternoon, he felt a little better. "Well, I'm not the only one stockpiling wood," he said as he hung up his coat. "There is nothing by the river, and much of the grove has been picked clean. I had to go a mile downstream before I found any wood, but I loaded up the cart. I've put a couple of stout tree limbs near the porch. Can you come out and help me stack the wood between them? That will give us a second wood pile." Virgie nodded and put on her warm clothes.

After they had emptied the cart, Papa lifted out four nice round stones. "Take these into the kitchen and pile them by the stove," he said.

"What are they for?" asked Virgie.

"When it becomes really cold, we'll heat them up on top of the stove and then put them in our beds to help us keep warm at night. I picked these up out of the prairie on top of the hill above the river, so they should work. We can't use river stones because they could have moisture in them, which would turn into steam when heated and then they could explode," he said. "With the weather we've been having so far, these might be welcomed."

After they put the last rocks in the kitchen, they warmed themselves by the stove. Papa looked around. "Where's Ruth?" he asked Virgie. "Getting ready for the party, I expect?"

Papa went out to hitch the horses up to the carriage. Virgie followed him out. "Papa," she said, "could I ride with you to take Ruth to the party? I don't go riding at night very often."

Papa looked down at her. "Well, I guess it wouldn't hurt. Sure. Put on your heavy clothes." The two girls climbed into the carriage and covered up with the thick buffalo skin robe as Papa drove to Mary's house. When they arrived, Ruth waved to a couple of other party-goers and hopped out of the carriage. Papa called out that he would be back in three hours.

As he and Virgie headed home, they heard shouts in the distance. Men on horseback overtook them.

"What's wrong?" Papa called out.

"The Sioux Falls stage tipped over at the river," replied one of the men as they rode past the carriage.

Papa turned to Virgie. "Are you warm enough?"

Virgie nodded. The buffalo robe nearly engulfed her in the back seat.

"I'm going to see if anyone needs help," Papa said as he urged the horses into a fast trot.

Men's voices grew louder and lanterns became brighter as they neared the accident scene. Virgie sat up straight and shoved away the buffalo robe. She didn't want to miss anything.

When they reached the riverbank, Virgie could see the chaos of milling people and neighing horses in the torchlight. Papa turned to her and said, "Don't leave the carriage. I'm going to see what I can do." He jumped down.

As soon as he had gone, Virgie climbed onto the front seat for a better view. In the light of the flickering torches, she could barely see Dr. Detrick attending to two men on the ground. It took her a few minutes to figure out who had been on the stage and who had come to help. She saw several men trying to calm the stagecoach horses, which were pawing the ground and snorting nervously. Finally, she spotted the stage on its side by the bank. But the top was gone. She thought she could make out in the dark the top of the stage where it lay on the ground.

When Papa returned, three people were with him. "These folks were passengers on the stagecoach," he said to Virgie. "Dr. Detrick asked me to take them to the Roscoe House hotel so they can be out of the cold. You stay up here with me, Virgie. We'll let them sit in the back and cover up with the buffalo robe."

Papa helped them into the buggy.

"I've never seen such a mixed-up mess," grumbled one of the passengers. "If our driver had driven more slowly down the bank, the stagecoach wouldn't have tipped over."

After delivering the passengers to the hotel, Papa and Virgie reached home at last. Virgie told Mama the story while Papa left to pick up Ruth.

On a Saturday late in November, Papa was up early and in the kitchen when Virgie came downstairs. He was dipping warm water from the five-gallon water reservoir on the side of the stove into a mug for shaving.

"Where are you going so early?" asked Virgie.

Papa turned and said, "We're going to raise the schoolhouse and place it on runners so we can move it Tuesday. Winter term should start soon."

Mr. DeBoer arrived at the door. He was also going to help raise the schoolhouse.

"Good morning," he said to Virgie before turning to Papa. "Mr. Mann stopped by yesterday and said we've had trouble receiving coal the past two months because the railroad companies are burning up all the available coal in their steam engines. He said Egan is having a 'fuel famine.' He also thinks there are people trying to monopolize the wood trade by controlling the shipments."

Papa nodded. "The local wood dealer says he doesn't have a steady supply of wood to sell because the railroad companies won't provide the cars to ship it here. But that's not true. The local railroad agent told me that anyone wishing to ship wood can have all the cars they want. We've had only two carloads of wood in the last six weeks.

That wood was half-rotten, and the price of $7.25 a cord was outrageous. Something needs to happen. We have to have fuel for this winter."

Virgie stood quietly with a bowl in her hands. What had she just heard? What did that all mean? Could her family die if they didn't have fuel? Would they freeze to death? She shuddered. Then she thought that these were problems facing all the villagers.

The next day after church services at Latch's Hardware Store, Virgie didn't see the Latches. She noticed how somber the grown-ups were as she overheard bits and pieces of conversation.

"There was another blizzard in Minnesota on Friday."

"The railroads are blocked again."

"I wonder if there will be coal or wood on the next train."

As they walked home, Virgie asked Papa, "Is it true about the train? Is it true we don't know when we'll have more fuel?" He had a grim look on his face as he nodded yes.

On Monday, the temperatures plummeted to minus fourteen degrees.

Monday, November 22

Virgie woke up shivering. She reached down for her quilt and found she had all the covers pulled up to her chin, but they were not enough. The round stone in her bed at her feet was icy cold. Any heat coming up through the hole cut in the floor above the cook stove was no match for the freezing temperatures that had invaded the upstairs.

She was shaking as she quickly put on her flannel undergarments, heaviest woolen leggings, and dress. They were ice cold. She wrapped the quilt around her and went down to the kitchen.

"It's cold everywhere," Papa said. "The thermometer read fourteen below at sunrise. We do seem to be having an early winter. Maybe it's time to buy a hog and have it butchered at the meat market. We can bury the meat in those snowdrifts on the north side of the house. It would stay frozen all winter."

The next morning was even colder, twenty degrees below zero. Virgie was glad there was no school so she didn't have to venture out in the freezing weather.

She was working in the kitchen after breakfast when she heard a knock on the door. She opened it and was surprised to see Lottie standing there. A frozen tear sat on Lottie's cheek.

"Lottie, come in," Virgie said as she grabbed hold of Lottie's hand. She pulled her friend inside the door and quickly shut it against the cold. "What is wrong?" she asked, pulling out two chairs at the table.

"Pa and I are leaving on the train tonight," Lottie said. "Ma wrote and said she won't come back to the territory. She said life is too lonely out here and too hard on a family.

She also misses her friends and relatives in Faribault. Pa sold the hardware store and our house yesterday to Mr. Paulson. The station agent said the track is open again."

Virgie had dreaded this for months but was not prepared for it this morning. "Oh, no!" she gasped.

Lottie reached over and gave Virgie a hug. "I'm going to miss you so much, Virgie," she said, tears spilling from her eyes. "But I've missed Ma and the boys terribly. I want us to be together again as a family."

Virgie nodded. She couldn't talk. Her throat felt tight. She was trying hard not to burst into tears. Finally she was able to say, "I really am happy for you, Lottie. I know I'd be terribly lonesome without Mama and Ruth." She took a breath. "I don't know what I would have done all summer without you."

"I wouldn't have gone out of the house after Ma left if you hadn't been with me," Lottie said. "Ma says we can write each other, and next summer you could take the train and come visit."

"That would be great fun," Virgie said, already excited at the prospect.

"Can you come help me pack the rest of my things?" Lottie asked.

Virgie looked at Mama, who nodded. She came over and gave Lottie a warm hug. "I'm very happy you're all going to be together again," she said. "You and Virgie have been wonderful friends. You can keep that friendship through letters."

Then Mama hugged Virgie. "Don't worry about chores, Virgie. Do you need a ride to the depot tonight?" she asked Lottie.

"No, thank you," Lottie replied. "Mr. Paulson has his wagon at the house. He'll help Pa load the household things, and then he'll take us to the train."

Virgie put on her coat, hat, and mittens, and they ran over to Lottie's house. They first packed Lottie's things and then helped her father in the kitchen. As the late afternoon sky darkened, Virgie knew she had to say goodbye.

"Here," said Lottie, pointing to a pile of folded fabric. "They're the doormats I made. We won't need them. I know you'll find a good use for them. Mr. Paulson will drop them off at your house on the way to the depot. And here, I want you to have this," she said, handing Virgie a small silver bell with a delicate bone handle. The clear, sweet chime hung in the room as Virgie carefully took hold of it.

"Oh, thank you," she said. "It's beautiful. I'll keep it forever. Goodbye, Lottie," she said, hugging her friend. Virgie quickly ran out the door before Lottie could see the tears streaming down her cheeks.

Virgie was still crying when she walked into the kitchen at home. She turned to her mother. "Why do people have to move? My only friend here, and now she's gone. Why did we have to move? It's not fair," she said angrily. "I want to move back to Sioux Falls so I can play with the twins."

"Now, now," Mama said. "Let's talk about it." She set a cup of hot cocoa on the table. "Moving is hard, both for those who leave and those who stay behind," she said as she sat down also. "Be glad you and Lottie were in Egan at the same time so your paths could cross. We want to make our life here in Egan, not in Sioux Falls. There will be more people moving into Egan, and you'll make new friends."

"When?" asked Virgie.

"When school starts, I'm sure," Mama replied.

"But they haven't even moved the schoolhouse yet," Virgie said.

Mama poured herself some more coffee.

Virgie stirred her cocoa. She had stopped crying. Finally, she looked at Mama. "I want to give Lottie something to remember me. Could I give her my silver thimble?"

"That's a good idea. You did a lot of sewing together," Mama said. "After dinner Papa can walk you to Lottie's."

As Virgie and Papa neared Lottie's house, they could see her father and Mr. Paulson loading the wagon. Virgie looked at Papa and said, "I don't want to stay long. I want to just give her the thimble and leave, or I am going to cry again." Papa nodded.

Virgie went up to the open door and called for Lottie, who came out. "Here, I want you to have my thimble to remember our good times," Virgie said as she thrust it into Lottie's hand. "I hope the tracks aren't blocked by snow and that you have a safe trip. I am glad you are all going to be together again. Goodbye." The two gave each other quick hugs, then Virgie was out the door and running ahead of Papa to her home.

Wednesday, November 24

The next day, Virgie had little time to think about Lottie. It was the day before Thanksgiving.

"Virgie, why don't you come grocery shopping with me? Ruth can run over to the DeBoers and see if they would like to join us for dinner tomorrow," Mama said. Virgie and Mama walked to the stores and started buying groceries. Ruth soon found them at the store and said that the DeBoers would be delighted to come.

"Good," Mama said. "I'll buy a nice-size turkey. We have parsnips and potatoes in the cellar. And we have cranberries. Ruth, why don't you check for oysters? Virgie, find a good pumpkin for the pies."

Virgie found a nice orange pumpkin. They paid for the groceries and the three returned home.

Ruth cut the pumpkin into thick slices, removed the seeds, and pared the outside. After cutting the slices into small pieces, she put them with a little water into a large pot on the back of the stove so they would slowly cook and soften for making pumpkin pie.

Virgie broke up the bread for the dressing and set it out to dry. Then she started cooking the cranberries for the cranberry tart pie. When the cranberries burst open, she added sugar and mashed them smooth. Mama rolled out the puff pastry, lined a pie plate with it, and cut strips of pastry to put across the top. Virgie poured in the cranberries and put on the pastry strips, then Mama put the pie in the oven.

By the time Virgie had finished her tasks, she was tired but excited that the DeBoers were going to share this Thanksgiving feast. She wished it were Lottie and her family coming. The DeBoers couldn't take Lottie's place, but they would help make the holiday cheerier.

The next day, Virgie heard sleigh bells jingle outside the kitchen door. She ran outside to find the DeBoers calling out greetings as they climbed down from their carriage. They had attached sleigh bells to their team of horses. "We thought a festive day deserves festive bells," Mary said.

Virgie felt very grown-up to be visiting with Ruth and Mary that afternoon.

"I have an idea," Ruth said. "Let's put on a little performance for our parents." The three huddled together in the parlor and decided to sing autumn songs.

Before dinner, the girls staged their performance. Virgie concentrated on singing the melody as she listened to Ruth combine her lovely soprano voice with Mary's rich alto. They concluded with a second singing of the autumn verse of "The Rain, Wind and Snow."

> "Wind, wind! Autumn wind! He the leafless trees
> has thinned.
> Loudly doth he roar and shout: Bar the door and
> keep him out.
> Wind, wind! Autumn wind! He the leafless trees
> has thinned."

Virgie smiled as their parents applauded loudly. She felt very thankful for her sister and family and their friends.

"That was wonderful," said Mama.

After dinner, the DeBoers left and everyone pitched in to clean the kitchen. Virgie went into the parlor to read her book from the twins. The heat from cooking made the room quite comfortable, she thought.

Mama and Ruth sat down at the kitchen table. "What a wonderful day," Ruth said. "Thank you for including the DeBoers. They are fun to be around."

"Papa and I really enjoyed the performance. You know, Ruth, you have been given a remarkable talent with your voice," Mama said. "Aunt Maud said you were thinking of teaching music. You could share your gift and help children. "

Ruth said she would also love to perform. "I'll probably have to leave Egan and move to a big city. Teachers in the territory have to teach everything. They can't have just one subject," she said. "But that's still a couple of years away."

1880

December

Christmas on the Prairie

Wednesday, December 1

Papa came home late again. Virgie and Ruth were just finishing the dishes.

"Hi, Papa," said Virgie as she opened the door to the warming shelf above the stove. "Here's your supper. Were you busy again?"

Papa washed up and sat down. "This week has been remarkable. I thought I couldn't do better than Monday, when I bought twelve hundred bushels of wheat. But that pace is keeping up. Since the teams can cross the river on the ice, farmers have been coming here instead of Flandreau. I've been buying their wheat. Roscoe Mill has been grinding it. I heard there were twenty-five teams at the mill, standing and waiting for grain to be milled into flour.

"Oh, I almost forgot. The train brought three carloads

of wood today. And the mail," he said, grinning. He pulled a letter from his pocket and gave it to Virgie.

Virgie let out a squeal of delight as she opened the letter. "It's from Lottie!" she said quickly. She started paraphrasing it to her family. "Lottie's train was stuck once on her way to Faribault. They had to wait two days for the track to be cleared. She's thrilled to see her mother and brothers. She said Willis has grown up and is talking a lot. She's busy unpacking and will write more later." Virgie looked up. "She sounds so cheerful. I really am happy for her." Virgie immediately went into the parlor to write her back.

On Friday, Virgie asked to go grocery shopping with Mama so she could mail letters to the Carnahan twins, Lottie, and Aunt Maud.

When they reached Third Street, both Virgie and her mother were surprised to see so many people standing in small groups outside the stores and more faces peering out of storefront windows. "What do you suppose they're looking at?" she said to Mama. As they walked to Barnard's store, Virgie could hear pieces of conversation.

". . . train cars carried 14 horses, 14 head of cattle, and 36 hogs."

"You wouldn't believe all the machinery he shipped here for his farm."

". . . the best hotel in town . . ."

They walked into Barnard's. "What's going on?" asked Mama.

"Mr. Johnson, the man from back east who's building the new hotel, just arrived by train," Mr. Barnard said. It had taken five train cars to carry his hotel supplies, household goods, and a store building he bought in Iowa and had shipped here. In addition, he had cars for holding farm machinery and livestock.

The following Wednesday afternoon, Papa called through the door. "I need some help. The train today had three carloads of wood, and I bought a cartload before it was all sold."

The two girls grabbed their coats and ran out to help unload and stack the wood.

"This has been a really tough winter," Papa said as they ate supper later. "The tracks were blocked Saturday by another blizzard in Minnesota. This was the first train in four days."

Virgie asked Papa if he knew when they were moving the schoolhouse. "I hear it will be next week," Papa said. "They've hired a man to move it. Now they need to buy fuel for the stove. Some districts are delaying winter term because they can't find wood."

Papa and Mama were starting to have a busier social life. On Friday, they went to a dance at the Paulson house. The following Tuesday, they went to a meeting of the Egan Literary and Social Society in Mrs. Barnard's home. The early settlers had formed this society to gather, visit, and share news. They created bonds of friendship. All were invited to attend. Those hosting provided refreshments, and those attending would give a program, such as a book review or musical performance. The evening could also include dancing or cards. "I was surprised at the number of couples who live outside of the village who drove their carriages in," Mama told the girls the next morning. "Mr. Nelson and his wife said they would not have come in if we had not had clear skies. We all had a good visit."

"Did you have anything to eat?" asked Virgie.

"Oh, yes," Mama said. "Mrs. Barnard served 'after-dinner croutons,' triangles of toast spread with a butter and creamy cheese paste. You should have seen how quickly they disappeared. She also made her famous almond cake." Mama paused for a moment. "I really enjoyed the visiting and the delicious food. But I'm most excited about the committee reports. I signed up for the literary committee and will give a book report for the next meeting. Mr. Barnard promises to order new books, but for now we'll report on those we have in our homes. I'll do a report on Dickens."

Snow fell again on Wednesday and Thursday, driven hard by the prairie winds. Papa said the coal situation was serious. "Railroads are having trouble buying coal to run the trains. Officials say they'll haul coal to settlers in preference to any other goods. But if coal companies can't furnish the coal, trains can't haul it."

A more gentle snow fell Friday. That evening Papa asked, "Anyone want to go for a sleigh ride?" There was a flurry of activity as Mama and the girls found coats, mittens, and buffalo robes while Papa removed the carriage wheels and attached the sleigh runners. He fastened straps of large belly bells around the bodies of Pal and Dusty and two long strings of smaller bells along the poles to the sleigh. "I can't imagine a sleigh ride without their joyous sound," said Papa as he climbed into his seat. And they were off.

"This is just magical," Virgie whispered to Ruth as they snuggled under the buffalo robe. The clouds had cleared, and the light from the full moon flooded across the fresh snow, which sparkled and twinkled like the night stars. The jingling of the smaller sleigh bells and the deep song of the large bells carried through the crisp night air. Soon they heard the singing rhythm of other sleigh bells and the laughter and shouts of friends as they greeted each other. They called out greetings to the Barnards and Detricks as they passed their sleighs near the river grove. The moonlight cast long black shadows from the trees across the snow, and the sleigh runners crisscrossed the shadows, creating geometric patterns on the landscape.

Everyone was in a cheerful mood. Christmas was one week away.

Christmas Week

"The movers say the schoolhouse is all set!" announced Papa on Tuesday night. "It's northeast of Paulson's Hardware Store. Winter term should begin January third."

"That's wonderful news," Virgie said. "It will be so good to be back in class. I can't wait to see if there are some new students. I miss playing with Lottie."

Ruth agreed. "Mr. Nelson promised to spend more time on music next term. He plays tuba and knows villagers who play the fiddle and trumpet. He asked if Papa wanted to play in a band. It would be fun to have them come to school and play."

"Well, I could certainly play my trumpet," Papa said.

The next morning, Mama and the girls went shopping for Christmas dinner. At the meat market, they bought a wild goose. They picked up several pints of oysters and some mincemeat at Barnard's. Mama sent Ruth to Molly's Restaurant for ribbon candy and peppermint sticks.

Virgie put two small bottles of paint on the counter for her Christmas decoration project.

"What do you want with those?" Mama asked.

"It's a surprise," Virgie said with a grin.

Christmas Eve morning, she joined the others in the kitchen. Ruth stood near the stove beating a pan of fudge. Mama rolled piecrusts for mincemeat pies. "Can I work at this end of the table?" Virgie asked, setting down her things. "It's so cold in the parlor."

She opened the sack of dried milkweed pods she had collected late in the summer. As she dumped them onto the table, the pods popped open. Fluffy white seeds floated into the kitchen. The slightest air movement propelled them this way and that. "Oh, no!" cried Virgie, trying to push the pods back into the sack. Mama grabbed a towel and covered the mincemeat.

Ruth exclaimed, "What is this?" as white puffs floated by the fudge she was beating. She bent over the pan to protect its contents and quickly ran into the parlor to continue beating. Virgie and Mama frantically scrambled to gather up the floating fluff.

Virgie and Mama finally restored the kitchen to order. "Virginia," said Mama sternly, "why didn't you clean those pods before you brought them into the house?"

Virgie looked chastened. "I forgot," she said. "I was so excited about painting them."

"Well," said Mama, "you need to put on your coat and go out onto the porch to clean those pods before you do another thing." Virgie took her coat and the bag of milkweed pods and exited the kitchen. Outside she quickly popped open each pod along its soft side and, using her fingers, pushed the silky tufts with their seeds out to be caught by the wind.

She quickly returned to the kitchen with the clean pods, whose insides glistened with a pale sheen that contrasted with the rough gray exteriors. Virgie opened a second sack, her recent purchases. She pulled out a small brush and the two jars of paint, one gold and one silver. She carefully painted inside the pods, a gold rim on one, a silver star on the inside of another. Each took on a different design. When finished, she tied loops of thread to the stem of each pod, ready to hang on the Christmas tree.

That afternoon, Papa brought in a small bush from the riverbank. Virgie and Ruth hung her milkweed pod ornaments on the branches, transforming the bush into a beautiful Christmas tree. Virgie beamed as the family praised her ornaments. The mess in the kitchen had been forgiven. Ruth placed the star, cut from heavy paper, on top of the tree. "It's the perfect tree for our first Christmas

out here on the prairie," Virgie said. Just before bedtime, she and Ruth read aloud the story of the birth of Jesus from the family Bible.

On Christmas Day, the family awoke to a blizzard. The wind howled fiercer than ever, and the air swirled with snow. Mama started the goose roasting in the oven and the heat from the stove quickly started taking the chill out of the kitchen. Papa went out to feed and water the animals and clean out their stalls. He grabbed a pail of water with one hand and took hold of the rope with the other. He held on, his shoulders hunched up and his face tucked down into the collar of his coat as he struggled from the house to the barn against the frenzied whirling of the wind and the sharp, biting snow.

When strong blasts of wind and snow swirled through the yard, the barn disappeared from sight. Mama, watching from the window, said she was grateful he had that rope.

"I'm glad we're not going anywhere today," Papa said when he finally came in again. He walked over to the stove and clapped his hands together to warm them. "It's not safe out there."

After breakfast, they exchanged their gifts. Mama immediately pushed up her thick hair with the new tortoise shell comb from the girls. And Papa put his pocket watch in its new leather case.

Virgie gave Ruth colorful satin ribbons for her hair. Ruth gave Virgie a new set of pencils. Mama had decorated white handkerchiefs with her handmade lace for each of her daughters. Papa gave Virgie a new silver thimble and Ruth a new songbook.

"Thank you for the wonderful gifts," said Virgie, going over and giving each one a hug. "I love your lace, Mama. Papa, the thimble will always have such a special meaning for me."

The aromas of the roasting goose, sage dressing, and scalloped oysters signaled it was time for Christmas dinner. Ruth spooned mashed potatoes and parsnips into bowls. Mama unmolded the cranberry sauce and its brilliant red was reflected over and over in the polished prisms of the small cut-glass bowl.

As Papa gave the blessing, Virgie, in her mind, added her thanks for the food, her family, and the gifts. She loved this meal. Even though the menu was the same every year, for her it was as much a part of Christmas as making ornaments and opening gifts. She couldn't help missing Sioux Falls—the bustle of shopping, drinking hot chocolate with the twins, and going by the sleigh to church services—and part of her ached once again for her old life. But she had to admit, this had been a special Christmas.

Monday morning the thermometer read thirty degrees below zero at daybreak, but it was not snowing. After putting on their coats, Mama and Papa struggled through the drifts to the cellar door. Through a window, Virgie watched them shovel off the door and open it. They returned, each carrying a basket filled with vegetables. "That was difficult going today," said Mama.

The cold continued on Tuesday, and the snow and wind returned, billowing and scurrying, building even higher the drifts between the house and the barn. When Papa came back from feeding the animals in the barn, he had his tools and some lumber with him. "I've been putting this project off for weeks," he announced. "Today is a good time to do it." In a corner of the kitchen, he cut an opening in the floor over the cellar. He put hinges on the piece he'd cut out to create a trapdoor. Then he lowered himself into the cellar. "Could you please hand me that lumber?" he asked Virgie.

She handed down the boards. Cold air wafted out of the cellar into the kitchen. But soon Papa had built a ladder, and the next time the family needed supplies from the cellar, they wouldn't have to go outside.

The weather on Wednesday was, as Papa said, a "real stunner." From early morning until late at night the wind never slowed. It blew at gale strength, and snow whirled and whipped around the house. "We're staying in," Papa said. "It's too dangerous out there."

That evening, Mama said, "Let's do something special tonight. Virgie, bring up some ears of popcorn from the cellar. We'll have popcorn and milk for supper."

"My favorite meal," said Virgie as she opened the hatch to the cellar and climbed down the ladder. Mama popped the corn in a pan on the stove, sprinkled the popcorn with salt, and drizzled melted butter over it. Then she filled their bowls with fluffy popcorn and poured on the milk. They ate it with spoons. Virgie thought the dish was perfect when the hot popcorn took the chill off the milk, which seemed to enhance the flavor of the popcorn.

"Papa," Virgie said as they finished their meal, "would you tell us again about your time in Andersonville Prison during the war?" Virgie never tired of hearing of her father's bravery.

Papa pushed his bowl away and leaned forward. "We were living on the farm near Albert Lea when the war broke out. The family was originally from New York and adamantly opposed to slavery. After talking it over with my father, I decided to volunteer. On June 10, 1864, my regiment marched into Mississippi and was directed to Brice's Cross Roads at Tishomingo Creek." Virgie had noticed that Papa never talked about any of the war except Brice's Cross Roads, the battle that he said changed his life. "It's a date I will never forget," he went on. "The road was very muddy. We were marching under a scorching hot sun, and it was very humid. The ground was so thick with underbrush and small trees that the officers had to send their horses to the rear of the troops. But we were a mighty force, 6,500 under the command of Brigadier General

Samuel Sturgis. We heard that a Confederate division of 2,000 cavalry troops had been seen in the area.

"I'm still not sure exactly what happened. We well outnumbered the Rebels. Then suddenly we were in battle, and the Confederate forces were everywhere. When the day ended, there were thousands of casualties on our side. Many of my friends were lying dead or dying on the field. It was a terrible sight. The Rebels took me and more than 200 other Union survivors—first to prison in Cahaba, Alabama, and then to Andersonville in Georgia."

Virgie interrupted him: "Weren't you scared?"

Papa got up, poured a glass of water from the stoneware jug, and sat back down. "Yes, I was. I cannot describe how horrible the conditions in Andersonville were. There were days in prison when I wasn't sure I would ever see my family again. We didn't have enough food. The small creek that ran through the prison provided water for drinking and bathing, but it was downstream from the outhouses so the water was horribly contaminated. We had no shelter. We were out in the rain, the cold, the sun, the heat. More than half the men in my regiment who entered prison with me died. I escaped that fate, but somehow in those awful months I picked up the infection in my eyes that causes them to water and burn.

"Early in the war, I had hidden a 20-dollar gold piece inside my suspender seam. No one had found it. With it I was able to buy some food, mostly oatmeal, from some guards and others in the prison that kept me going. At the end of September, they sent some of us who were in the best physical condition to a prison in Savannah, and then two weeks later to Camp Lawton, near Millen, Georgia. We had heard that prisoner exchanges had been halted by General Grant, but for some reason there was an exchange at Millen, and I was one of the lucky ones. I was released November 26 and shipped to Camp Parole, Maryland. From there I received a thirty-day furlough and transportation money to take the train to Chicago, and then on to La Crosse, Wisconsin. I had to walk to Albert Lea from La Crosse. The family said I looked pretty awful coming up the road. Mother was thrilled. She had thought she would never see me again. After the holidays, I had to report back to my regiment and then was discharged in July of 1865.

"I regained back most of my health, but my eyes still flare up. But I was lucky. I met Aggie, and a few months later we were married."

Virgie fell asleep that night with images of her brave father walking out of the prison gate after surviving months of living without shelter and adequate food.

Friday, December 31

On four out of the previous five days, howling winds had battered Egan and sent whirls of snow skimming across the buried prairie. The house creaked and moaned as the timbers shifted from the force of the wind. The windows rattled with each blast. The wind whistled under the eaves and shrieked when it exploded off the roof. "I am so tired of that constant howling," Virgie said at supper. "I can never get away from it."

On Friday, the wind stopped. "Listen," whispered Virgie as she tiptoed into her sister's bedroom. "There's no sound. It's completely still outside. It seems rude to talk out loud and break the silence. The world looks so gentle."

She and Ruth looked out the window at the incredible landscape. It looked unreal. "The wind has sculpted the snow like whipped cream or beaten egg whites," Ruth said.

After breakfast, they put on heavy coats and helped Papa shovel a path to the outhouse, barn, and well. "Where are we going to put the snow?" Virgie asked as she looked at the snow-packed path. It was a channel through the drifts of snow, and in places it towered over the girls.

"You girls take the spades and cut out small blocks of snow from the path," Papa said. "I'll throw them up over the edge. I have an idea for the well," he added.

They cleared the path to the outhouse, and when they reached the well, Papa disappeared into the barn and returned with a barrel that had once held feed for the animals. He knocked out the bottom and banged and shook the barrel to rid it of any seeds or debris. "There," he said. "That looks clean enough." He walked up the snowdrifts, which were solid enough to support him, and placed the barrel over the opening of the well. "We can lower the pails through here to reach the water."

They tamped down the snow to the frozen pork and oysters buried north of the house. Those chores finished, he left to check on the warehouse.

1881

January

It Can't Get Worse, and Then It Does

Saturday, January 1

Papa arrived home that night holding a telegram and the newspaper. "The company wants my help for two weeks at the Pipestone warehouse," he said. "As soon as the tracks open, I'll leave."

"Two weeks?" Mama asked. "That's a long time to be gone in this weather. Will you have a good warm place to stay?"

"I'm sure I'll bunk in the warehouse office, and it will be good and warm," replied Papa. "I'll be fine." Then he looked at Virgie and Ruth. "I want you two to be on your best behavior. Don't do anything foolish in this weather. It's too dangerous."

Virgie and Ruth quickly nodded. "We'll be good helpers, I promise," said Virgie.

"Good," Papa said. He handed over the newspaper:

"There's a story in *The Egan Express* about admitting Dakota Territory to the Union as the state of Dakota. That would be good."

On Tuesday, the tracks reopened, and the first train in ten days arrived in Egan. "I bought a load of coal, which is out in the cart. I'm glad you'll have fuel while I'm gone," Papa said. "And you girls will be happy to hear this news. The school board hired a man to deliver coal to the school, which he has done."

Virgie and Ruth helped Mama replenish their supplies of sugar, canned oysters, molasses, cornmeal, dried fruit, and coffee beans. Virgie received letters from Lottie and the Carnahan twins. Virgie immediately opened them and quickly read them. "It's like reading my own letters," she said. "There is no school because of the storms. They are bored. Lottie has started piecing together a doormat for their house. The twins say there is talk about shortages of coal and wood in Sioux Falls."

Later that night, Virgie and her family hugged Papa as he left to board the 1:15 a.m. train east for Pipestone, just across the Minnesota border. The next morning they awoke to fresh flurries.

"Girls," Mama said, "before the snow worsens, please run down to the station and find out about your father's train. I'm going out to take care of the animals." The station agent told the girls the train arrived in Pipestone just ahead of the storm.

On the second day, the storm let up in the early morning, so Mama and Virgie headed to the barn. The fresh snow overnight had covered the path they had shoveled out and trampled down on their many trips to the barn. They had come out of the deep channel and were walking over drifts toward the barn when Mama slipped on the frozen snow and fell into a large drift and sank down into it. "Mama!" Virgie cried. "Are you hurt?" Mama shook her head but struggled to stand up. Her layers of petticoats and thick wool skirts weighed her down, and she could find nothing in the snowdrift to help pull herself up. The snow was coming down again, and it was heavy.

"I can't stand up, Virgie," Mama said. "I'm going to need some help."

Virgie turned toward the house and yelled for help. But the wind took her words and scattered them. Virgie peered through the blowing snow. "I see the rope Papa tied from the house to the barn," she told Mama. "Let's see if I can bring it to you." She pulled on the rope, and there was enough slack that it came close to Mama. "I have to move it closer," Virgie said. "Maybe my scarf will work."

Virgie unwrapped the muffler from her neck. She tied it onto the rope and held out the end to Mama. "Here, Mama," Virgie said. "Grab the scarf and pull. I'll pull your other hand." Both of them working together had Mama standing again.

They gave each other big hugs. "That was scary," Mama said. "I am so glad you were here to help me. How foolish of me not to hold onto that rope. I could see the barn but I forgot about the ice underfoot." Mama gingerly took a couple of steps and then said, "Let's finish the chores."

On the third day of the storm, Mama said, "We need to carry hot water out to thaw the water in the troughs. Virgie, you grab the barn rope with one hand and my arm with the other. I'll bring the pail of hot water. We'll refill the pail at the well on our way back."

The wind and snow blasted them as they walked out the porch door. "Hold tight!" Mama shouted to Virgie. "It's worse out today than yesterday." When they reached the barn, Mama quickly closed the barn door behind them. "We're not going to be able to clean the stalls completely because I'm not going to open those doors again until we go back to the house. Shovel the hay and manure into a pile at the back of the barn. I'll milk Bossy."

"Oh, yuck," Virgie said, wrinkling her nose as she saw the chickens pecking for seeds in the horse droppings. She shooed away the chickens so she could shovel up the manure.

On the way back to the house, they followed the rope to the well. They lowered the bucket and heard a clunk. "Oh, no," Mama said as she peered down into the opening. "The water has frozen. We'll have to fill the pail with fresh snow and melt it on the stove." Mama picked a new drift and scooped snow from it and took it to the house. "At least we have snow to melt."

The storm lasted three days, and with no word from Papa. Virgie noticed that the new wrinkle in Mama's brow didn't go away.

As soon as it stopped snowing, Virgie and Ruth put on their coats and said they would go to the post office. They held each other's hands to keep their balance and give each other support as they slipped and slid up and down the drifts to Third Street. At the post office, they asked if there was mail from Papa, but there was not. They came back with lots of news, none of it from him.

They knew Mama's first question would be about the trains. "There is nothing moving," Ruth said. "Mr. Paulson said there are 500 cars loaded with freight for the Territory between here and La Crosse. They shovel open one section, and the wind blows the snow right back in."

"And we learned something else," Virgie said. "School starts next week. But you should see the schoolhouse. It's not even."

"That can't be," Mama said, shaking her head.

"Virgie is right," Ruth replied. "It's set at an angle. Mr. Paulson said that another blizzard started when the men moving it reached the east edge of town. They and the horses were exhausted. They had to reach shelter, so they left the schoolhouse on those snow banks, and now it is frozen there. I wonder what it will be like to study."

The following Wednesday, Virgie and Ruth went to Mr. Paulson's store. "I know what you're looking for," he said with a smile. He reached down and pulled up two envelopes.

"Oh, thank you," said Ruth, quickly taking them.

The girls hurried home as fast as they could. As they neared the side porch, Virgie shouted, "Mama, Mama! The stagecoach came through. You have two letters from Papa." They ran into the house, gasping to catch their breath.

Wednesday, January 12

Mama quickly opened one of the envelopes and started reading.

> *My Dear Girl,*   *Jan. 6, 1881*
>
> *I'm sending you $5, but do not know when you will receive it as the roads are so bad, and it is snowing now like the d----l. We've had one train since I arrived here.*
>
> *Will be some time before we get another. I have had nothing to do. After it stops snowing, we will have some work to do to clean the snow off the grain in the warehouse. It has drifted in on the wheat, some places two feet deep. I feel uneasy about you and would like to be with you through this storm.*

Get a load of wood out of the money. At the end of
this week I will send you $10.

How are the children? I do hope they are well. After
we get the snow cleaned off the wheat, I may come down
if there is no prospect of trains.

With love to you and the children.

I remain, Your Loving Boy, Ben.

Mama smiled. "He sounds good. I wish there were
wood to buy." She opened the second letter and read it
aloud as well.

Dear Aggie,   Jan. 7, 1881

It is still snowing and I do not know when you
will get this. If it were not for cleaning snow out of
the warehouse, I would start for Egan on foot as I am
worried about you. This is the worst storm I've ever
seen—looks as though we are going to get to the 17 feet
total that everyone is predicting. I am in comfortable
quarters but keep thinking of you and the children. Of
course, I imagine everything.

Kiss the children for me and keep one for yourself.

Your Affectionate Boy, Ben.

Mama sighed. "I do hope he doesn't try to walk here. This
is the second time he has mentioned that. What if another
blizzard came up? He could become lost and freeze to death."

That night Mama went to the Egan Literary and Social Society meeting. The girls sat near the warm stove in the kitchen and read until Mama returned.

"The literary committee's report on Dickens' *Pickwick Papers* was well received," she said. "There were also two vocal solos and a quartet. The two men who gave a comb concert by blowing through tissue paper covering a comb were amusing," she said with a smile. "The next debate question will be 'Resolved that intemperance causes more unhappiness than war.'"

"What's intemperance?" asked Virgie.

"It's doing too much of something, like eating. But this question will be about drinking too much," Mama said.

She said that Mr. Mann said that statehood leaders now want to divide Dakota Territory in half and have Southern Dakota admitted as a state. Northern Dakota would stay a territory until its population grew.

"There was lots of good news discussed tonight," Mama continued. "It was announced that businessmen have donated a half block of land and $165 to build a Methodist Church. They are still seeking donations, as they say the church will not cost less than $1,200.

"Ruth, you will be glad to know Mr. Brower is starting a choir. He'll announce the time and location of the first practice in the paper. And Ole Olson is building an ice house," she concluded. "He said the sawdust for packing the ice is on its way from Wisconsin."

As they prepared for bed that night, they noticed snow falling again. Another blizzard blasted into Egan, and it was snowing and blowing wildly when they woke up in the morning. Mama asked Virgie to bring up some vegetables for soup from the cellar.

"It's really cold down there," said Virgie when she climbed back up. "Will the food freeze?"

Mama nodded. "If there isn't a break in this weather soon, that's very possible. Some of the vegetables will spoil and we won't be able to use them."

Friday, January 14

That night, they planned to go to the schoolhouse for an oyster stew supper being held by the literary society. The general stores had received good supplies of canned oysters with the last train. Mama had volunteered to bring a large kettle of stew.

Virgie decided to write Lottie. "I can't wait to go to the oyster stew supper," she wrote. "I have nothing to . . ." Her writing was interrupted by Ruth laughing in the kitchen.

Virgie walked into the room as Ruth said, "I have a message from Mrs. Barnard. They've canceled the oyster stew supper. Wait until you hear why! The schoolhouse is so uneven that soup won't stay in the soup bowls. It will spill 'over the western horizon,' as she put it."

Virgie burst out laughing. In her mind she saw little oysters smiling as they escaped with the liquid pouring over the sides of the bowl as if over a dam. That vision, she thought, was almost worth not being able to go to the supper.

Then Mama turned to smile at the girls. "Guess what we're having for supper tonight, tomorrow, and the next day?"

Sunday afternoon, Ruth went to visit Mary and quickly returned home. "Virgie," she called as she walked in the door. "Get dressed. They're ice skating on the river. Let's go!"

They quickly put on layers of woolen stockings, skirts, and coats. "I've waited all winter to go ice skating," Virgie said as she dressed. Mary's father picked them up in the sleigh and drove them to the river. There the wind had blown clear the snow from a nice-size area for skating. A dead tree trunk on the opposite riverbank had been set ablaze. Virgie could see skaters warming their hands and feet by the fire.

"This is going to be so much fun," Virgie said to Ruth. She fit the blade plate to her shoe and tightened the skates' clamps on to the leather soles of her shoes. The leather straps from the skates came up over the tops of her shoes, and she buckled them tightly.

"Let's go over to the fire," Mary said to Ruth.

"No, wait a minute," Ruth said, standing up. "Do you see what I see? Look at those two boys skating on the new ice formed where Mr. Olson cut blocks for his icehouse. That is really dangerous. That ice is too thin to skate on."

"You're right," Mr. DeBoer said. He ran down to the riverbank. "You, boys!" he shouted to them. "Move away from the icehouse. That is thin ice. It will give way and you'll fall in. Come back!"

The four watched as the two boys turned and walked on their skates through the snow to the cleared ice. "That's better," said Mr. DeBoer to the girls. "The ice there is two and a half feet thick, and it is safe."

"I know who those boys are," Virgie said. "Danny and Joey Thompson."

"Let's skate over to the fire," Ruth said. She and Mary took off. Virgie called over her shoulder, "I'll meet you there. I'm going to skate around the circle."

She was skating slowly, trying to make sure her skates didn't come loose and fall off her shoes, when two skaters whizzed by her so quickly she almost fell.

The skaters spun around, and she heard Danny say, "There's Spider. Let's get her."

Danny and Joey skated toward her, and she took off. She skated directly across the circle toward the bonfire. She knew she was at a disadvantage. Her long heavy skirts did not allow her to skate nearly as fast as the boys. She was almost across when they caught up and skated circles around her, taunting, "Seen Mr. Miles lately?" Danny's brown eyes sparkled under the mop of dark brown hair that poked out from his knitted cap.

Virgie stopped, put her hands on her hips, and said, "Just stop that, Danny Thompson. It was your fault you got caught, not mine. Now, leave me alone. And stop calling me Spider."

Laughing, the boys skated away.

Exasperated, Virgie skated on with great determination. She was so angry at them she forgot to watch the ice as she neared shore, and she tripped on the frozen, rippled edges. Her skates tore away from her shoes, and she landed face first in a snowbank.

Ruth skated over as Virgie came up sputtering and spitting snow. "Are you okay?" Ruth asked.

"Thank you. I'm fine," Virgie said. "But Danny Thompson is a horrid boy."

Monday, January 17

Forty-four boys and girls came to school that morning. All the students agreed it was good to be back. Everyone had been extremely bored the past few weeks. Many made jokes about having trouble standing up straight in the slanted school.

"Welcome back to winter term, scholars," Mr. Nelson said. "It's obvious that we have a problem with the school sitting unevenly on its site. It's getting quite the attention. Did you see the letter to the editor about it?" he asked, opening up a copy of *The Egan Express*. "The writer, who signed the letter 'Citizen,' wrote, 'Editor Express: Would it not be an improvement to the external appearance and to the internal convenience of the schoolhouse to have the off side raised to a level with the near side? Also, to make the house front the street instead of the alley, and its necessary appurtenances. Will the Board kindly consider the matter?'"

Mr. Nelson lowered the paper. "That was a well-written letter," he said. "Perhaps when the weather clears, they can jack up the school building with some supporting lumber or move it. For now, we'll have to make the best of it."

He started seat assignments. Turning to Virgie, he said, "I have new a desk mate for you." Calling to another student, he said, "Polly, come meet Virgie."

Virgie watched Polly cross the room. Red curly hair tumbled below her shoulders.

"Her family came in on the last train two weeks ago. They're staying at the rooming house waiting for their household goods to arrive," Mr. Nelson said. "Her father, Samuel Nussbaum, is the new station agent here."

"Hi, Polly," Virgie said, and the two girls walked to their assigned desk. "We're going to have to hold onto our desks to keep from sliding off." While Mr. Nelson assigned the rest of the students to desks, she and Polly got to know each other. They laughed over the story of the canceled oyster stew supper.

Finally Mr. Nelson had assigned all the desks. "We're going to be packed in," he observed. "No single desk assignments this term." Some of the youngest scholars were sitting three to a desk. Virgie was glad to see Danny seated on the far side of the room.

"With forty-four students it's going to be a challenge to do a good job of teaching all of you," Mr. Nelson said. "I am going to ask Mary to assist me with the youngest children. If you need help, Mary, ask Virgie. She is ahead on her studies. And I'll talk with Ruth about setting up some music lessons she could teach."

Then Mr. Nelson cleared his throat. "I have been told that a couple of boys were overheard swearing in one of the stores. If you don't already know this is wrong, I will tell you that it is. In addition, under the laws of Dakota Territory, every swearing is punishable by a fine of $1. Remember that. It could save you a good deal of money."

Virgie and Polly exchanged looks. *I have an idea who those boys are,* Virgie thought.

As the students left the school that day, she asked Polly if she would like to come over and make rag dolls. "It could be a good project," she said. They could give the dolls to the youngest girls at school. Polly said she would love to. "The rooms of the boardinghouse seem to grow smaller each day," she said. "It will be good to be in a different room."

When the girls reached home, Mama had good news. She had another letter from Papa. Virgie turned to Polly and said, "Papa is working in Pipestone. We can work on the dolls as soon as we read his letter." They quickly took off their coats and gathered around the kitchen table.

Dear Girl,   *Jan. 17, 1881*
Still no trains. The prospect is poor for having one before spring. It has been snowing fast since last night. Clyde and I are having easy times. We've done nothing today but sit around and swap lies. Will have nothing to do until the train gets here. Warehouses are full. I send with this $5. How are the children? I hope they are all right.
    Two mill workers here, Mr. Wagner and Anthony, went out to shovel snow. They got tired of it and started to walk to Flandreau, 15 miles away. They came near freezing to death. Wagner had one side of his body and feet frozen. Anthony both of his feet. They didn't get into Flandreau until after dark. It took them over two hours to go the last mile.
    With love to my Girl and Children.
    I remain, Your Affectionate Boy, Ben.

"I'm sorry to hear about Mr. Wagner and Anthony," Mama said. "But maybe they showed Papa the folly of trying to walk anywhere in this weather."

Another letter arrived the next day. Papa said the company was bringing in a fresh crew every two weeks, and as soon as the new work group arrives he will leave on the next stage.

Virgie was looking out her bedroom window the next day when she saw a familiar head bobbing up and down behind the snowdrifts. "Papa's home!" she cried as she ran downstairs.

He was smothered in hugs at the door.

"They pulled a crew from near Pipestone," he said. "I left just after I sent the letter. How is everyone? It's good to be home."

Thursday, January 27

Virgie was even more thankful he was home when another blizzard threatened on Thursday. When he walked into the house that night, he was waving a copy of *The Egan Express*. "Look at this," he said. "It's printed on wrapping paper. Mr. Mann said he's printing on anything he can find. His newsprint is on a train east of the snow blockade in Minnesota. So is wood for fuel."

He pointed to the wrapping paper. "Mr. Mann has two interesting articles about the blizzards," he said.

Ruth took the paper and read aloud: "'For the past six weeks we have had very severe winter weather, in fact the worst that has been known in this country for years. Blizzard has succeeded blizzard so closely that it has been hard to determine when one ceased and another commenced. During the time mentioned, but three or four trains have reached this place owing to the blockade in Minnesota, east of Fulda.

"'As soon as the wind would cease blowing and the snow flying, the railroad company commenced to open the road but would scarcely get the track clear ere the wind again filled the cuts with snow.'"

Ruth stopped. "The second story is about the fuel shortage," she said. Then she read: "'Wood! O, would to God that the trains would get through and bring some wood, is the cry of the average Eganite. Several carloads of wood are on the road consigned to parties at this place, but the Lord only knows when it will get here.'"

Papa and Mr. Mann were both talking about the fuel shortage. Virgie knew it was serious.

Mama said they had burned most of the purchased coal. They would soon start burning the wood Papa had scavenged from the woods earlier in the fall.

"Not good," Papa murmured. He looked at Virgie. *This is a scary conversation*, she thought. *What if we run out of fuel? Could we freeze to death? The twins wrote about fuel being short in Sioux Falls, but it couldn't be this bad. Maybe I could talk Papa into moving back to Sioux Falls.* Virgie's mind was racing. *How could we get back there? Not the trains, because the tracks are all blocked. Our horses and carriage probably couldn't get through the snowdrifts on the trail. Could we take a stage back to Sioux Falls? No. We would be really cold in a stagecoach. Oh, no. We are literally stuck here.*

Virgie slumped down in her chair.

Then Papa changed topics.

"On a happier note, the band is starting practice this weekend." He grinned. "Eight of us are committed to play. There are some pretty good musicians here. I'm looking forward to it."

That Saturday night, Mama and Papa went sleighing with friends. Two sleighs pulled up outside the door, and Mama and Papa climbed in. Virgie and Ruth waved goodbye and listened to the peals of laughter float like musical notes through the sharp night air.

The next morning, Papa found his old spear in the barn. It was a sturdy willow branch with one end notched and sharpened. "What's that for?" Virgie asked.

Papa held the spear in the air and felt its balance before replying. "Last night, folks said there's good spearfishing in the river. They described how they were spearing through the open water where Mr. Olson is cutting ice for his icehouse. With any luck, we'll have fresh fish tonight."

"Oh, that sounds like fun," Virgie said. "I like to fish, but I've never gone spearfishing. Could I help you? Could I ask Polly to go too?"

"Of course," Papa said.

Later that morning, Papa, Virgie, and Polly walked with three neighbors to the river where the ice was being cut. "Here," Papa said. He handed each of the girls a tree limb. Two of the men stood by the hole of open water while Pa, Virgie, Polly, and Mr. Paulson used their sturdy tree limbs to hit the ice as they walked upstream. The fish headed downstream away from the heavy thuds toward the other two men, who speared them as they swam past the ice hole. Then those two men took the

branches and beat the ice while Papa and Mr. Paulson waited at the hole. "Here come the fish," Virgie and Polly called out together as they peered into the hole. Papa and Mr. Paulson speared the fish as they swam through.

"This is unbelievable," Papa said as he strung the perch on a line. "I've never done anything like that before." He sent a portion of his share home with Polly. They had fresh fish for dinner.

1881
February

"Winter of Perpetual Elemental Fury"

Tuesday, February 1

Virgie was amazed at how busy her parents had become. It seemed to her they were always going to literary society meetings, debates, dance socials, sleigh rides, or band practice.

"We should have a dance social here Saturday, February 5, to celebrate Virgie's birthday the next day," Papa said Wednesday night. "Hank Block plays a good fiddle. A couple of us in the band could toot some tunes."

"Oh, yes!" Virgie exclaimed. "That would be such fun. I'll invite Polly."

"We'll have to plan," Mama said to Virgie and Ruth. "Nobody will expect much in the way of food since supplies are so scarce. But we'll have a cake for you, Virgie."

"It's good for the people to be together and have fun," Papa said. "There are so many reasons to be in a grim mood these days. Wood is scarce. The food shelves at the stores are becoming emptier. It doesn't look like we'll have a train anytime soon. Do you realize the last one was two weeks ago? Thank heavens we still have wheat for flour and frozen meat."

Wednesday, February 2

Virgie heard the icy darts of sleet beating a staccato against the schoolhouse windows. She looked up and wondered if it were yet another blizzard. Within minutes, she had her answer. The wind turned the snow into a full assault on the tiny village. Mr. Nelson wasted no time. He went to the door and stepped outside for a moment.

Back inside, he told the students to prepare to leave. "It's going to be bad. I'm not going to ride out to my claim," he said. "I'll stay at Mrs. Cummings' Rooming House." He told the Anderson children and the Peterson boys to come with him and wait in the living room for their parents, who would know where to find them in this bad weather. Polly would walk with them also. "Those who live in town, go directly home," he concluded. "Don't dawdle."

They all understood the dangers of a blizzard and being lost on the prairie. It was not a time to take chances. When winter term started, Mr. Nelson had set very strict rules for blizzard days.

"I remember when we used to cheer the arrival of the snow," Virgie said to Polly as they bundled up. "We couldn't wait to go out. But now I am tired of the cold and snow. The only place I'm really warm is in the kitchen."

Noah Peterson turned to her and said, "I know. We can't keep the snow out of our shanty. It comes in with the wind. Every morning Pa has to shovel out the snow by the door and windows, and I have to shake the drifts off my blanket."

Virgie looked at the small six-year-old with his patched jacket and pants. He wore no cap, and his mittens had holes in each thumb. "Can't your mama put an old blanket in front of the door?" she asked.

"We don't have any old blankets," Noah said. "We have them all on our beds."

"Shush," said his eight-year-old brother, Luke. He turned to Virgie. "We're just fine. It's no problem shoveling out the snow. We're plenty warm."

As the children walked out the door, the snow hit them with a fury. Icy beads stung their faces, and the wind seemed to blow right through their coats. Virgie took one last look at Noah and Luke, huddled over as they walked with Mr. Nelson toward the rooming house. Luke had no mittens at all, and his thin jacket had as many patches as Noah's.

Virgie caught up with Ruth, who had waited for her. They knew they had to walk together during storms. With their heads bent down to avoid the blowing snow, they trudged home.

Papa was already there. "It looks like a bad one,"

he said. "The farmers who brought in grain turned right around and headed home."

The girls brushed the snow off their coats and hung them up. The family sat around the kitchen table and told one another the news from their part of the village.

Papa said the bill to admit Southern Dakota as a state was defeated by the House Territorial Committee. "There's no chance for statehood for at least a year now."

Mama looked at Virgie, who had remained uncharacteristically silent during all of this talk. "What's wrong, Virgie?" she asked.

"I'm worried about Noah and Luke Peterson," Virgie said. "I don't think they have much money. They live in a drafty shanty without much to keep them warm in this horrible weather."

"That's too bad," Mama said. "There's not much they could do if they did have money. The stores are sold out of the heavy clothing. And sewing a quilt for them would take a while."

Virgie looked at her mother. Drafts. Patches. Quilt. "Oh!" she shouted. "I have an idea. Wait." She ran upstairs to her bedroom and pulled a box out from under her bed. She pulled out the six doormats she and Lottie had stitched and made six trips down and back up the stairs, carrying each mat to the kitchen.

"What have you there?" Mama asked. The family stared at the pile she had put on the table.

"Doormats that Lottie and I made," Virgie said, unfolding one of the thirty-by-seventy-two-inch panels. She told them about seeing the old clothes in Mr. Mann's office and the project she had proposed.

"Lottie made hers to keep out drafts. I practiced my stitches. When Lottie left, she gave me her mats. I was so sad that I hid them under my bed so I wouldn't be reminded of the fun we had. I could give these to the Peterson boys, and they could hang them in front of their door and windows. They're big enough that Noah and Luke could put them on top of their beds, too."

Mama said, "I saw you sewing the patches together, but I didn't know you had turned them into doormats. You even padded them."

"We did that at Lottie's house when her father was working," Virgie explained.

Mama picked up a mat and examined the stitches. Virgie handed her the other two. Mama was silent for a moment. "Yes, I can tell that this was the last one you finished. Beautifully done," she said fingering one of them. "That is a generous offer to give these to the Petersons," she said, looking at Virgie. "What do you think, Papa?"

"It's a wonderful idea, Virgie," he replied. "But how do

we take them out to their place? I have no idea where they live, and it's too stormy to go out on the prairie now."

"The boys went with Mr. Nelson to wait for their parents at Mrs. Cummings' Rooming House. We could take them there," Virgie said. Then she hesitated. "I'm not sure how happy Luke will be. He didn't want Noah to tell anyone they were cold."

"I have an idea," Mama said. "Papa can talk privately to Mr. Nelson at the rooming house. He could tell the Petersons that a traveler had left the mats there and that Mrs. Cummings had no use for them. The children will not have to know they came from you."

Virgie nodded. "Yes, that'll be good."

She helped tie up the mats as Papa put on his heaviest coat. "You stay here, Virgie. It's too stormy for you to be out."

"And," Mama said, smiling, "I think it's time for you to learn to make lace."

Mama and Virgie looked up from their sewing when Papa returned from his trip. "It went well," he said. "Those doormats will be put to good use."

For the next three days, Virgie watched the wind drive the snow swirling and skimming across the snowpack, with occasional eruptions of snow into the air as the forces collided. Each day she hoped that the storm would stop so they could have their party on Saturday. But on February 5, she awoke to the blizzard still howling. She was surprised to find herself more resigned than disappointed at the decision to cancel their party. She knew it was not safe for anyone to be out.

After supper that night, Mama took the cover off the cake plate and brought a white fruitcake to the table. "My favorite," Virgie said, beaming. "But how could you make it when the trains haven't come in? Where did you buy the citron and almonds? And the figs?"

Mama smiled as she sliced the cake and passed it around. "I have my secret hiding places in the pantry," she said. "I bought the ingredients before Christmas."

Ruth handed a small wrapped package to her sister. "This is from all of us," she said.

Virgie carefully removed the wrapping paper so it could be used again. The gift was a book—a collection of poems by Henry Wadsworth Longfellow. She gently caressed the gray cover scattered with purple violets. She looked up at her smiling family. "This is a wonderful present," she said. "I'll keep it forever. Thank you."

Papa cleared his throat. "Another case of shopping early."

As Virgie curled up under her quilts that night, she thought of her birthday. "I am now eleven years old. Today was really special," she said to herself. "My family is really special. Last December, Mama was already planning for my birthday and buying the ingredients for the cake."

Virgie stopped thinking of her party for a moment. "Mama didn't just plan for my birthday. She was preparing for winter. We could have run out of food if we had not done all that work."

The next day Papa came home early for supper. He said the railroad had put out a call for all able-bodied men and boys to help shovel out the tracks so the trains could get through. "Businesses have closed so men can help clear. I'll be gone several days. Everybody's worried. There's no wood for sale anywhere. We have maybe one week's supply left."

Three days later Papa returned home. His eyes had started watering again, and then snow blindness set in. Several others had it too, he said.

Later that evening, Virgie overheard her parents talking in the kitchen. "Things are not good, Aggie," Papa said. "I don't think the track can be shoveled out. The drifts are immense, forty to fifty feet in the deep cuts. And it's packed almost as hard as ice. There's not a mile of road on the entire line that doesn't have to be cleared of snow before the trains can move. Any wind covers the tracks right back up. I wouldn't be surprised if the railroad just gives up trying to clear the tracks."

Mama looked at him. "What's going to happen?" she asked. Virgie stood quietly in the shadows, listening for Papa's answer. The conversation was frightening.

"This weather could last another four to six weeks." He

caught sight of Virgie listening in. "Even if we wanted to give up and return to Sioux Falls, we couldn't. Everything is snowbound." For some, it could become desperate. No food. No fuel. People in Watertown had pulled up railroad tracks so they could use the ties for fuel. A couple of bridges were torn down for their wood. Some families were burning their furniture.

Mama sighed. "I don't have good news either. The vegetables in the cellar are frozen. I can make frozen potato soup. It's not tasty, but it is something to eat. And we still have the frozen pork, flour, eggs, and milk."

Papa picked up the newspaper and said, "The headlines tell the story: 'Terrible Times. Railroads Badly and, it is Feared Effectually Blocked. Scarcity of Food and Fuel in Many Places. Storm after Storm adds Terror to Despair.' "

Then Papa read the story: " 'The present winter has been such a one as few of our hardy settlers have ever experienced, and such a one as all pray to never again witness. Since the middle of October, winter has reigned supreme. Since that time storm has followed storm in such rapid succession that it might almost be called a winter of perpetual elemental fury.' Well said."

Virgie went back upstairs and, with tears in her eyes, told Ruth what she had heard. "There's no wood. What will we do?"

Ruth said, "It is scary. But trust Mama and Papa. They'll know what to do."

That night, the temperature dropped again. The cold came right through the walls. When Virgie dressed in the morning, she decided to put on as many layers of her flannel undergarments, wool leggings, and wool skirts as she could. "What is wrong?" she mumbled. "These aren't tight on me anymore." She pulled on a second wool skirt. "And I can fasten this one over the other. Instead of growing bigger, I am getting thinner." When she went into the kitchen, she told Mama her observations.

"I'm not surprised," Mama said. "We've all lost weight. I certainly notice it in what I'm wearing. And I just don't have the energy I did earlier this winter."

That week, another blast of snow and wind closed any tracks that had been opened. As the family's wood supply dwindled, they burned some of the corncobs they had dried. When the cobs were gone, Papa brought stacks of straw from the barn into their living room and showed the girls how to twist small bundles of it into hard knots they could burn in the stove.

"We're not the only ones doing this," Papa said. "Lots of folks have run out of wood and are having to burn straw knots. When these are gone, we'll bring in the dried cow pies. I'm glad we have a stack of those chips."

School continued, which gave the girls something to do. "It's boring being snowbound, and now it's scary that nobody has any wood," Virgie said to Polly during lunch. "Last summer my life changed so much when we moved here, and the town changed every day. I didn't like it. But I'd rather have change instead of constant snow and cold and nothing to do."

That night, she took down her teapot and pulled out her secret calendar. She put down another mark and then started counting the total. She came to thirty-nine marks, one for each week since their move. *My goal is fifty-two marks. I don't think it will ever come. We are going to be burning cow chips for fuel, the food in the cellar has frozen, and I am losing weight. I'm scared.*

Thursday, February 24

On their way home from school, Virgie and Ruth saw Mr. Mann crossing the street.

"Hello, girls," he said, coming over to them. He showed them a copy of the newspaper. "Notice the wrapping paper I'm using for newsprint? I'm getting papers from editors in other towns who are printing on cloth and wallpaper. Three weeks ago I sent the Dell Rapids editor my paper printed on just one side. Yesterday I received it back with his latest edition printed on the back. That was the first mail from the south we've received in two weeks. And I can't remember the last time we had mail from the east."

He looked around at the snow-covered village. "We've had at least seven feet of snow since October 15. There must be a good four feet on the ground now, not counting the drifts."

Virgie was not surprised at his next statement. Mr. Mann always found the good in anything. "When all the snow melts, it will soak into the ground, and our farmers will have a big crop next season! I really can't find anybody who is discouraged by the hard winter. They all have the grit and backbone that Dakotans need."

Then he gave the girls a huge grin. "You can tell your papa my prediction that we'll have a train through by July 4. He'll want to go to the celebration."

Virgie relayed the joke to Papa that night. He laughed and said, "Yep, I'll be there."

1881
March

A Life Saved

Friday, March 11

Papa had heard that the trains would be running again in two weeks. "Then we're going to have to watch the river," he said. "There's a good chance it'll flood. But we can't do anything about that now."

When Virgie awoke the next morning and saw snow falling, she knew what kind of day it would be. A foot of white, granular snow fell, and she was snowbound again with nothing to do.

"No, no, no," she cried Monday morning when she looked outside. She saw snow falling as well as old snow blowing wildly about. There was no school. "I'm so tired of this winter. I want it to end. Now!" she said, stomping down to the kitchen.

"You're not alone," Mama said. "Why don't we make some lace today?"

"I'm even tired of that. I'm tired of writing letters. I've read all our books at least three times. I'm tired of everything," she said with a pout. "And my feet hurt. My shoes are too small."

"I'm not surprised that you've outgrown your shoes," Mama said, "but you know as well as I do that there are no new ones in the stores. Now, why don't you go sit in your room and not spread your bad mood around. We are all tired of this winter. Think how you can make the best of it."

Virgie went up to her room, wrapped herself in her quilts, and sat. After an hour she came back downstairs. Being housebound with nothing to do had happened too many times over the winter, and this time she decided she was going to do something about it. "I have this idea," she said to Mama. "When there is a lull in the storm, could I walk to the rooming house and ask Polly if she wants to exchange books for a couple of weeks? I've read my new Longfellow book twice and *Andersen's Fairy Tales* so many times I can read the stories without looking at the words. I could let her read those if I could have a couple of her books to read."

Mama thought that was a good idea. "Ruth could walk with you," she said. "Perhaps Polly's parents have a book or two they would like to exchange with Ruth. She could take one of my Dickens books to trade."

Virgie and Ruth bundled up, grabbed the books, and walked the two blocks to the rooming house. Polly ran down the stairs and came into the living room to greet them. She thought a book exchange was a wonderful idea. She brought down several books, including one for Ruth, who immediately sat down at the desk and started reading. Virgie and Polly sat on the rocking chairs in front of the fireplace and talked.

"Did you see Thursday's newspaper?" Virgie asked. "Mr. Mann printed our school report scores! We three all had above 90 in proficiency and deportment."

"How embarrassing it would be to have a low score printed in the paper for everyone to see," said Polly.

"I know," Virgie said. "Danny and a couple of other boys had a 60 in deportment and low 40s in proficiency. Their parents couldn't be happy about that."

Thursday, March 17

Mama and the girls struggled through the snow to buy flour at Barnard's.

"I can only sell you fifty pounds," Mr. Barnard said. "Flour is getting scarce. The Flandreau mill isn't grinding wheat anymore. The Roscoe Mill can grind only a few hours a day because the water in the river is so low. I've had customers from Flandreau come and carry the fifty pounds home on their backs." Mama paid for the fifty pounds and said Papa would come in later to pick it up.

Trains were predicted to reach Egan sometime the following week. But when the time came, there were no trains.

Virgie's mood was lifted by the arrival of a soft, southerly breeze. "Feel that air," she said to Polly as they left school. "There's a lightness to it. It'll soon be spring."

Polly didn't share those thoughts. "I just want to move into my own house," she said. "I want a train to arrive with our belongings. It seems as though I'll live in that rooming house forever."

Tuesday, March 22

Virgie awoke to the groaning of the house timbers. Wind and snow hammered the northwest corner of the house, and it creaked and groaned in return.

She quickly dressed and went downstairs. "Do you know there are little snowdrifts in the corner of my room?" she said to whoever would listen. "I think the wind just pounded the snow right through the wood."

"I know I'm telling you the obvious, but there's no school today," Papa said.

"This is not fair. There's just one week left of this term," she said, pouting. "I am so tired of this weather."

"It is frustrating," Papa agreed. "I think this is the worst blizzard we've had this winter—and we've had a lot of them! I don't think the wind has ever been this fierce. The railroad company almost had the tracks open. Trains would have been here by Saturday night. Now it will be at least another week."

On blizzard days, Mama would ask the girls if they wanted to bake a treat to brighten the afternoon. "What can we make today?" asked Virgie.

"No more treats," Mama said. "The popcorn and sugar are gone. Papa and I are stirring hard candies into our coffee to sweeten it. And I have to save the flour for bread."

Virgie knew flour was scarce, but they did have some wheat. She helped Mama make it into flour in the coffee grinder. Mama hovered over the grinder, hoping the gears wouldn't break. Virgie didn't think the flour tasted as good as that from the mill.

The storm stopped early Wednesday morning. Papa started for work but quickly returned. "The lanes are impassable. You won't be going to school either," he said to the girls.

Yet another blizzard hit Saturday morning. But on Monday, the girls finally returned to school, walking by towering drifts, many over ten feet tall.

Virgie was disappointed to hear Mr. Nelson say there would be no program at the end of term because the weather was too uncertain. As Virgie and her sister left school with Polly that final afternoon, snow started to fall. "This is the third storm in a week," she said to Polly. "I bet this means no trains."

As had become their practice, Polly joined Virgie and Ruth in the walk home. She liked having a house to go to rather than the rooming house, and Virgie was delighted to have her friend come to play. They were well on their way to making a nice supply of rag dolls to give away.

Suddenly they heard what they thought was a howling sound in the distance. They froze.

"Could that be a wolf?" Virgie asked with concern in her voice.

"I'm glad I'm walking with both of you," Polly said as she grabbed hold of Virgie's arm. They hurried on to Virgie's house. The howl sounded closer when they heard it again as they ran onto the porch and into the kitchen.

"Did you hear the wolf?" Mama asked. The girls said they had. Virgie and Polly went upstairs to Virgie's room to find fabric they could add to their rag dolls, and then they heard the sound again: a long, eerie wail. They walked over to the window and listened again. "I don't think that is a wolf," Virgie said.

"It didn't sound like one that time," Polly agreed. They listened even more closely at the window.

"No," Virgie said. "I think that is someone calling for help." When they heard it again, Polly agreed.

"Someone is hollering for help," Virgie said as they ran down the stairs. "We need to help him." The two girls grabbed their coats and the lantern. Virgie's mother and sister looked at them with doubtful eyes.

Virgie and Polly opened the door.

"Wait," Papa called. "Let me get my shotgun just in case it is a wolf. There have been two reports of wolves in the area."

But Virgie and Polly were already out in the yard. They stopped and listened. They heard the sound again.

"Over there," Virgie said, and the two girls ran, following the sound. They followed it behind the barn. There they found a man lying in the snow moaning for help.

Virgie took off her coat to cover the man and said to Polly, "Quick, tell Papa we found someone, and tell Mama and Ruth we need their help."

As Polly ran off, Papa came around the corner and added his coat to the man. His beard and mittens were frozen hard and his fingers and face were gray. Polly soon returned with the rest of the family. The man's joints were stiff from the cold and he had trouble trying to walk. Together they were able to lift the man and carry him into the warmth of their kitchen. They piled blankets on him, and Virgie poured him a cup of hot coffee.

"Who are you? Where did you come from? How did you get behind the barn? How long were you there?" The questions flew at the man, who gradually regained the ability to talk as he warmed up.

"Thank you for finding me," he said. He told them he was Henry Oliver, and he had been traveling from Madison to Flandreau on business when he became lost. He had spent the previous night in an abandoned sod shanty, and then he started out again this morning. He said that after an hour of walking, he found himself back at the shanty. He had walked in a circle. He started out again, found the railroad track, and ended up on the edge of Egan, behind Vandenberg's barn. There, he collapsed, exhausted and freezing cold. He said he pushed himself to start hallooing when he heard voices in the distance coming closer. He knew he would freeze to death if no help came.

Papa went out and hitched up the horses to the carriage and took the man to the rooming house where he could safely spend the night. Polly rode with them to be with her parents. "I am so glad you are safe now," Polly said to Mr. Oliver.

"Good job, Virgie," Papa said on his return. "Mr. Oliver is alive because you recognized his call for help, and you found him."

1881

April

Pasque Flowers Call

Tuesday, April 12

Virgie walked into the house, her shoes muddy. She had gone to see Polly and found it a messy trip. "But I'm glad the snow is melting. Mr. Paulson built a sidewalk in front of the hardware store," she told her mother. "That makes two sidewalks. They are so nice."

Mama agreed. "I'm glad it's warmer, but I hope the snow doesn't melt too quickly. The river will never be able to handle it. Nobody seems to know whether the village is on high enough ground or if it could end up flooded."

Monday, April 17

Virgie came into the house calling out, "Mama you should go down and see the river. The water is almost to the top of the riverbanks. The river looks so angry."

Mama looked up from her sewing. "You weren't down at the river by yourself, were you?"

"With Polly," she said.

Mama shook her head. "It's becoming way too dangerous. I don't want you and Polly near the river unless Papa is with you. Understand?"

Virgie nodded.

Papa walked in the door that night wet, muddy, and tired. He sat down before he spoke. "Well, we've done our best. Ice is jammed above the railroad bridge. The water on the east side is washing out the track. We've tried to shore up the bridge. I'm not sure we can save it."

He paused, letting his fingers smooth his mustache. "Another group went down to the highway bridge and tried to tie it up. The miller had a workforce driving piles into the ground above the mill to divert some of the flow." He described how large vertical columns of wood were pounded deep into the ground to support the bridge and train tracks. The wooden piles also formed a barrier to the river, forcing the water to move around them. "We'll see if anything works," he said.

Virgie stayed away from the river after that. As the river grew in size, she became scared of its dark whirling waters, large bobbing ice chunks, and floating tree trunks. The river overflowed its banks and flooded the bottomlands, but so far, the town was still dry.

On Saturday morning, Virgie walked with her family to the east edge of town and looked toward the river. She saw water everywhere. The bare branches of the tallest trees in the grove rose above the churning water. As she watched, a tree was ripped up by its roots with a crashing sound, and it washed away with the gushing water. And there were the frequent sounds of large ice chunks banging into trees floating in the river. "That river's gone from two hundred feet to more than a mile across. It looks more like the Mississippi River," said Papa, awestruck. The river was twenty feet over the level of the water during the dry season.

Mr. Nussbaum and Polly walked up to the little group. "Did you hear?" Polly asked. "The highway bridge was swept away this morning. It stopped about a mile downstream. And the ice house is gone."

"Oh, no," Papa said. "The farmers won't be able to bring their wagons into Egan. They'll go to Flandreau, and we'll lose their business."

Looking up the river, Virgie noticed the ice building up behind the bridge. The bridge groaned and began to move. She let out a shout: "The railroad bridge!" Everyone turned to watch as the ice and water reached higher and raised the heavy iron bridge up and off its piles. The metal bridge supports gave a wrenching sound as the sections of the bridge buckled and then crashed down into the river. The force as they hit the water lifted slabs of ice the size of wagon beds high into the air, and then they came back down.

Virgie's initial shout started a crescendo of cries from the gathered crowd. "The railroad bridge! The bridge is going!" Their voices followed the bridge as large sections of it bobbed up and down on the surface of the river and found their way among the ice blocks in the channel. The bridge scraped against rocks, making the bend just east of town where it came to rest.

"Oh, we'll never have another train come into town," Virgie cried, tears welling in her eyes.

Papa put his arm around her shoulders. "It's certainly not what we'd like to see," he said. "It's another delay, but there will be trains again. I'm going to go check the pilings."

When he returned, he said the good news was that the pilings were still in place. "We can put the bridge back after the water goes down." Then he let out a rare, frustrated sigh. "The trains were so close! They were at Pipestone Creek this morning and expected to reach Flandreau tonight or tomorrow. We could have had trains in Egan tomorrow night."

Papa repeated the news he had heard from businessmen and townspeople who had congregated along the river. They were already talking about plans to keep the town moving forward. A ferryboat large enough to carry a team and loaded wagon across the river was going to be built from wooden remnants of the bridge that would be gathered up as soon as the water level dropped. Work on the highway bridge itself would start as soon as possible.

"The good news for me is that the mills here and in Roscoe are still standing, so farmers can bring their wheat to my elevator to be stored or to those mills to be ground," he said. "Unfortunately, the Flandreau mill didn't make it." The family took one last look at the river and headed home.

The Sioux River rose no higher, and in a few days, it started to recede. Monday afternoon, Papa came home early. "Put on your oldest shoes and boots," he directed. "We're going to pick up firewood." As they rode to the bottomlands in the cart, Virgie saw other villagers searching the wet ground. The dank smell of water and mud-soaked wood filled the air. Tree limbs, branches, building frames, siding, broken bridge planks, and railroad ties littered the ground, all left behind by the floodwaters. She and her family gathered the pieces up until their cart was full, and then they went home to dry off.

Tuesday, April 26
As temperatures warmed and the early grasses started turning green, Virgie's spirits improved. She and Polly

walked to Third Street to check on the mail and found good news. Mr. Paulson and Mr. Smith had rowed a flat-bottomed boat down the river to Dell Rapids and brought back all the Egan letter mail—the first mail from the south they'd received in a long time.

The sun was drying up the mud on Third Street, and there was a general bustle to the area as merchants readied their stores for new shipments of goods, which would be coming in on the first train in four months. Those who were out and about moved freely as they were not hindered by the weight of heavy coats and hats as they had been just weeks earlier. "Even the clothing worn by people on the street really changes how the street looks," Virgie said to Polly.

The girls stopped in at Papa's warehouse, where he was buying oats and wheat that farmers had stored over the winter. "They launched the ferryboat this morning, and these are the first wagon teams to come across from the east side of the river," he told them between customers.

As the girls walked home, Virgie said, "I didn't think winter would ever end." She stopped and sniffed the air. "Do you smell it?" she asked Polly. "I can smell the earth warming up. Spring is really coming." With that she put her hands up in the air and started twirling down the lane. Polly joined her, and they spun circles until they collapsed in laughter in the field across from Virgie's house.

As they rolled over to stand up, Virgie leaned down and pushed aside the dried blades of last year's grasses. "Look," she said. "These pretty lavender petals are pasque flowers. My favorite sign of spring!"

A week later, Virgie heard shouts: "It's coming! The train is coming!" She looked out her window and saw men running down the lane shouting.

"Let's go," Virgie said to Mama and Ruth. "I want to see it come into town."

They hurried to the tracks where townspeople were lined up. Virgie and her family joined the crowd at one end and leaned forward to look down the track. The tiny plumes of smoke gradually grew larger as the locomotive and twenty cars came into view.

Virgie could not believe she was finally seeing a train. For months, she had heard Papa say the train was coming and then not coming, coming then not coming. Now she heard everyone cheering and clapping. She waved to the train's engineer when he leaned out the window.

Everyone was walking the length of the train looking in the cars. The town's shop owners drove their wagons and carts up to the tracks to load new merchandise for their stores. "My newsprint is in the sixth car," Mr. Mann called out.

Polly ran up to Virgie. "We've got our things," she said

excitedly. "We're moving into our house tomorrow! You'll have to come visit and see our home."

"Yes, ma'am," Virgie heard a crew member say. "There are carloads of wood. And plenty of supplies. These cars have been sitting on tracks in Wisconsin for months."

As Virgie turned away from the tracks, she saw Danny and Joey with their parents walk out of the sidecar depot.

"Hi, Danny. Hi, Joey," she said. "Did you have a shipment come in?"

"No," Danny said. "We bought tickets to go back to Illinois. This winter was too hard."

"Oh," Virgie said. "Well, goodbye . . . and good luck." As she walked away, she smiled to herself and thought *I did it! I outlasted Danny and this winter.*

She and Ruth walked over to Papa's warehouse. They told him about all the train cars that had pulled in.

"I've heard there are three hundred cars on these tracks and sidings," Papa said. "I believe it. I think cars will be arriving here for several days."

Monday, May 9

Now that stores were restocked, Virgie and Ruth couldn't wait to help Mama shop. She hitched the horses to the cart, and they drove to Third Street. They crowded into the stores with other shoppers. Virgie didn't even mind the jostling, tight squeezes, and noise. Finally, she found a spot where she could see the shelves filled with clothes, crockery, glassware, pots, fabric, and all kinds of groceries.

They found new hook-and-button shoes for Virgie and Ruth, a shaving brush for Papa, and gingham fabric to make a new work dress for Mama. Virgie lost count of all the different groceries Mama put on the counter to buy. They filled Papa's order for house paint. And they bought a supply of wood that a clerk stacked in their cart. Virgie felt a surprising sense of relief knowing that

there was wood and that she would be warm on rainy spring days.

Soon, their cart was filled with supplies, so Mama drove it home while the girls walked. Once there, they started unpacking the cart and stocking the pantry.

During a break, Virgie went upstairs and took the lid off the little teapot and pulled out her secret paper calendar. *Well*, she thought, *this paper served me well. Marking off the weeks helped me go through some tough times—the move here, leaving Catherine and Carrie, no friends, Lottie leaving, blizzards, boredom, fear of no fuel. It has almost fifty-two marks now and I don't need to add any new ones. I can throw this away. I belong here.* She tucked the paper into her apron and went back downstairs.

As she walked into the kitchen, she recognized a new feeling: *I am really proud of making it through this year.* She pulled out the paper, carried it to the stove, put it into the fire, and watched it blacken and curl in on itself. As it disappeared, she thought of how she helped the Peterson boys and Mr. Oliver. She thought of her new best friend, Polly. She remembered packing to leave Sioux Falls one year ago, and she didn't know if she would recognize that girl she was.

Mama walked into the room. "That must be an interesting fire," she said. "You're sure staring hard at it."

"I was thinking," Virgie said. "I realize that I like it here. I was so disappointed when we arrived and there was no town. Now it's hard to remember when there was nothing here. Mr. Mann was right. We really did see the birth of a town. Now it's ready for its first birthday."

Author's Note

The story of Virgie and her family is fiction, but it is based on a real family: My own great-grandparents moved to Egan in 1881 with their two daughters. The family photos, letters, and recipes that add richness to Virgie's family's story are based on real items that have been passed down to me. The same is true of other items, such as the autograph book, silver bell, Seth Thomas clock, Virgie's tiny doll, her toy tea set, and sleigh bells. Like Pa in this story, my great-grandfather was a grain buyer in Egan, and he was imprisoned in the Confederacy's Andersonville Prison. The letters that Pa writes to his wife during that winter of horrible blizzards are actual letters written by my great-grandfather. Even the report on birds that Virgie reads at the school program is authentic: It was written by my grandmother as a child in Egan in 1884.

A critical resource in my writing was the town newspaper, *The Egan Express.* I was able to obtain original copies of the *Express* for the years 1880–1881. And yes, some of them were printed on plain wrapping paper. The newspaper that year had two editors, each for about six months. Each editor reported weekly detailed accounts of the growth of the tiny village and was supportive of it. I was taken by their enthusiasm. How do you build a town from nothing on a harsh Dakota prairie? What was life like for those early settlers?

No one knew that summer as they moved to Egan that the approaching winter would be so challenging and even life-threatening for them. Blizzard came on top of blizzard so closely that it was difficult to tell when one storm ended and the next storm began. Food and fuel were in very short supply. The editor of *The Egan Express* called it what it was: "a winter of perpetual elemental fury."

The Girl Who Moved to the Town That Wasn't There is an accurate account of those historical events. It does not describe how settlement might have happened. It tells the reader of events that are true and did happen, based on more than 260 articles from *The Egan Express.*

Other sources for the book included pioneer cookbooks and school books, old photographs of the area, and visits to Andersonville Prison, Brice's Cross Roads battleground, and historic frontier villages. Incidental information on everyday life in 1880 has been verified by interviews with Dale Johnson, Moody County historian; Linda Hasselstrom, South Dakota author and rancher; Robert Kolbe, Sioux Falls historian; and several texts on pioneer history in Dakota Territory, all of which are listed in the bibliography.

The story of how Egan was founded is incredible and inspiring to me. I wanted school children to know the struggles and the spirit that went into building the small towns that dot our maps. To make it fun, I told it as fiction through the eyes of a young girl. To make it substantive and authentic, I relied heavily on all these sources.

Bibliography

Publications

Bragstad, R.E. 1967. *Sioux Falls in Retrospect.* Sioux Falls, SD. p. 2.

Coates, Henry T. 1879. *The Children's Book of Poetry. Carefully Selected from the Works of the Best and Most Popular Writers for Children. "The Rain, Wind and Snow."* Philadelphia. Porter & Coates. p. 306.

The Egan Express, W.S. Cobban, editor. Volume 1. June 3 to Oct. 14, 1880, Numbers 2 to 14. Egan, Dakota Territory.

The Egan Express, Geo. R. Lanning, editor. Volume 1. Oct. 21, 1880, to May 1881. Numbers 26 to 52. Egan, Dakota Territory.

Frey, Hugo, editor. 1935. *America Sings. A Community Song Book. "Tramp! Tramp! Tramp!" (written 1864)* Geo. F. Root. Robbins Music Corporation, p. 109.

Johnson, Dale, and Duncan, Anna. 2010. *Echoes of Egan. Photo History of Egan, South Dakota 1880–2010.* Flandreau, SD. Moody County Historical Society. p. 15, 78.

Kirkpatrick, Mrs. T.J. 1883. *The Housekeepers New Cook Book. Embracing Nearly One Thousand Recipes and Practical Suggestions to*

All Young Housekeepers in Regard to Cooking and the Utensils Used. Springfield, OH. Mast, Crowell & Kirkpatrick. p. 7.

Kreidberg, Marjorie. 1975. *Food on the Frontier. Minnesota Cooking from 1850 to 1900 with Selected Recipes.* Minneapolis, MN. Minnesota Historical Society Press. p. 60, 61, 64, 66, 73, 74, 81, 91, 94, 95, 101, 115, 116, 151.

Longfellow, Henry Wadsworth. (nd); *Poems by Henry W. Longfellow. "The Village Blacksmith."* Chicago. M. B. Donohue & Co. p. 195.

Luchetti, Cathy. 1993. *Home on the Range. A Culinary History of the American West. New York.* Villard Books. p. xxxiii, 23, 27, 41, 114, 123.

Nobles County Historical Society, Pioneer Village. School house tour.

Van Bruggen, Theodore. 1983. *Wildflowers Grasses and Other Plants of the Northern Plains and Black Hills.* Interior, SD. Badlands Natural History Association. p. 12, 17, 20, 27, 41, 53, 74, 75.

Wentworth, George Allen. 1889. *Grammar School Arithmetic.* Boston. Ginn & Company. p. 26, 75.

Ziemann, Hugo (Steward of the White House), and Gillette, Mrs. F.L. 1901. (copyright 1887) *The White House Cook Book. A Comprehensive Cyclopedia of Information for the Home.* New York, NY, Akron, OH, Chicago, Il. The Saalfield Publishing Co. p. 217, 277, 284, 347, 556, Chapters on Cake and Pastry, Pies and Tarts, and Sauces and Dressings — Salads.

United States Military War Records. US Microfilm M546, Roll 10.

Brochures
Andersonville, National Historic Site. Georgia. National Park Service. U.S. Department of the Interior.
Brice's Cross Roads and Tupelo. Mississippi. National Park Service, U.S. Department of the Interior. National Battlefield Sites.

Interviews
Hasselstrom, Linda. Author, Poet. Hermosa, SD. Windbreak House Writers Retreats. October 2011 and May 2013.

Johnson, Dale. Director, Moody County Museum. Flandreau, SD. Interview November 15, 2011. Conversations June 25, 2013 and January, 2020.

Kolbe, Robert. Author, Historian. Sioux Falls, SD. Interview October 31, 2012. Conversation August 2, 2013.

Web Resources
Faribault Heritage Preservation Commission,
 http://faribault pc.org
First United Methodist Church History:
 http://sfumc.org/about/history
Template Talk: Omaha Railroads: Wikipedia
Victorian Rag Curls:
 www.youtube.com/watch?v=t7bjCSteybc

Family Items

Vandegrift, Thomas Hart Benton. 1881. Letters to his family. In author's possession.

Vandegrift, Virgie, Report on Birds. In author's possession.

Family heirlooms. Candleholder, Seth Thomas clock, small doll, child's tea set, silver bell with horn handle, sleigh bells, GAR pin, Longfellow book, autograph book, photos of Virgie and Ruth.

About the Author

Suzanne Hovik Fuller has been a writer for her entire career. She was an award-winning staff writer and consumer investigative reporter for the *Minneapolis Star* from 1964–1975, and she taught reporting at several colleges from 1977–1982. She also served in many leadership roles as a community volunteer for several non-profit organizations that served children, families, and the arts. Suzanne is a native of Sioux Falls. Her love of South Dakota is deeply rooted in her experience of the land, walking the fields during hunting season and nurturing native prairie, and in her ancestors whose graves she still places geraniums on in Egan's Hillside Cemetery. *The Girl Who Moved to the Town That Wasn't There* is Suzanne's first book.

About the Illustrator

Emmeline Forrestal, a Wisconsin native, grew up loving tales of prairie life such as the Little House on the Prairie series and Caddie Woodlawn. After graduating from the University of Wisconsin-Stevens Point with a degree in Theatrical Costume Design, she moved to Minneapolis where she worked for many years at the Guthrie Theater. While living in Minneapolis, she became interested in illustration and worked on many books for Book Bridge Press. She recently moved to California where she works part-time as a children's library technician and full-time as an illustrator. When she's not drawing, she can be found spending time with her family, reading, and thinking about drawing.